Praise for Rick Cochran's Books

Wellfleet Tales and *Wellfleet Tales II: Confessions of a Wash-Ashore* – "The chapters have a funny and familiar ring ... colorful stories in helping us recall a distinctive time and place on our small peninsula." **Barnstable Patriot**

"In *Wellfleet Tales* and *Wellfleet Tales II: Confessions of a Wash-Ashore,* Rick Cochran reflects on what it was like growing up in the Outer Cape town of Wellfleet during the 1950s and 60s. A retired teacher, Cochran paints a picture of a simpler time. … Written with tenderness, detail and an obvious passion for the subject matter." **Cape Cod Life Magazine**

"Rick Cochran is a wonderful writer who knows his Wellfleet, the subject of his three books. He understands the dynamics of a small town: how a story can catch fire and that there are things that must be said... and things that must not be. Fortunately, he says them all here. In the course of his engrossing tales and his mystery novel, we see the inner workings of a tight-knit community, one that may exist now only in memory. And while not everything is idyllic in the world he has created, it is all animated by affection for the place and a canny understanding of its people." **D.B. Wright, Author, *The Famous Beds of Wellfleet: A Shellfishing History***

"During a recent winter power outage, Cochran's wonderful writing kept me turning the page along with a flashlight and headlamp. *Murder at Bound Brook* turned out to be a great read."
Barbara Eppich Struna, Author, *The Old Cape House, The Old Cape Teapot, The Old Cape Cod Hollywood Secret*

"This well-plotted mystery is one of the best I've read in a long while. The author is more than familiar with Cape Cod, so the background settings and description are first-rate. But what held me was the clever plot that had me guessing until the very end. The murderer could have been a young man as well as an old man, or other suspects in between. Added to this, is a love interest that has been rekindled, a marriage on low flame, high school basketball teams of young people trying to find their way, and a police chief who has not been embraced by the community. If you are looking for something a little different but gripping, *Murder at Bound Brook* is for you."
Ray Anderson, Author, *The Trail, Sierra*

"If you enjoy a story that captures the flavor of the setting, then you are going to love *Murder at Bound Brook*, Rick Cochran's first novel. He knows of what he speaks, having grown up on Cape Cod and knowing first-hand life in a small Cape Cod town."
Steven P. Marini, Author, *Connections, Aberration, Calculation, Henniker Secrets, Schmuel's Journey*

Also by Rick Cochran

Wellfleet Tales

Wellfleet Tales II: Confessions of a Wash-Ashore

Murder at Bound Brook: Cape Cod Mystery

(also check out my Facebook group, "Wellfleet

Tales")

Bound Brook Pond

Cape Cod Mystery II

The story continues

by

Rick Cochran

Rick Cochran

This is a work of fiction. References to real people, events, establishments, organizations or locales are intended only to provide a sense of authenticity. All other characters, incidents or dialogue are drawn from the author's imagination and should not be considered as real.

Richard Cochran

Bound Brook Isle Publishing
Hull, Massachusetts 02045
2020
wellfleethigh@outlook.com

Cover Design
By
Rick Cochran

ISBN - 9781070276014

Dedication

To all the people, past and present, who love Wellfleet and the Outer Cape. To my wife, Ellen Keane, the best thing that happened to me – love you.

"Men at some time are masters of their fates. The fault, dear Brutus, is not in our stars, but in ourselves…"
William Shakespeare – Julius Caesar

Author's Note

In the legends of Scotland, as well as on Broadway stage and movie screen, the magical village of Brigadoon appears to mortals one day every one-hundred years. For ninety-nine years, you can search for Brigadoon; it will be there, but you will not see it. The fictional hamlet of Bound Brook, Cape Cod, exists only in my novels; it is my personal Brigadoon.

In the real geography of Cape Cod there is an area known as Bound Brook Island. It was a small settlement within the town of Wellfleet. At its height, the village had sixteen homes, a schoolhouse, salt works and whale watchtowers. Duck Harbor and the Herring River provided a navigable port. Its most famous native son, Captain Lorenzo Dow Baker, became the "Banana King" and brought tourism to Wellfleet with his Chequesset Inn.

Duck Harbor and the Herring River became victims of the constantly changing coastline of Cape Cod. They began to fill with silt and today they are merely marshes. By the early 1800s, the village was fading and by the end of the century it was virtually abandoned, many of its houses hauled to Wellfleet Center. Now, it is uninhabited.

However, could it be that, like Brigadoon, it is still there just beyond our view? Are the Lombards, Hopkins, Higgins and Bakers still roaming its dense woods and shrubs searching in vain for the village that they knew? Maybe *my* Bound Brook is what would have happened if that tiny hamlet had somehow prospered and grown into its own incorporated town.

My Bound Brook gives me the freedom to create a world like the town where I grew up in the fifties and sixties. It allows me to fabricate characters and slip in a few real-life cameo appearances. It lets me create crimes, tragedies, love and loss. My mind is free to wander through familiar territory while my imagination creates fanciful drama.

For the most part, people and places in the towns of Wellfleet and Provincetown who appear in my books are real and existed in 1952. I have endeavored to cast these real people in the most positive light. I hope that for them, their children, grandchildren, friends and families it will be fun. Their appearance is a small tribute to the adults I knew and the positive influence they contributed to my town and to me.

The residents of Bound Brook, however, are a different story. They are imaginary, and like the illusory chimera of mythology, they flicker in and out of focus, as an amalgamation of different people, real and imagined. They are players in my stories and fulfill their roles to further my plot. They are flawed heroes, nasty villains, tradesmen, teachers, soldiers, sailors, mothers, daughters, fathers, sons, young and old; in other words, they are like the folks in most any rural town.

Someday the Bound Brook residents may materialize from the murky pages of my fiction to walk the beaches, hollows and dunes of Cape Cod. Yet, like Brigadoon, it will be at least another ninety-nine years; by then perhaps you and I can appear from those same foggy mists and join them.

In the meantime, I hope you will enjoy your trip to the village of Bound Brook, Cape Cod, Massachusetts.

Contents

Part One: The Villain

"O villain, villain, smiling damned villain."
William Shakespeare – Hamlet: Act 1, Scene 5

"Tut, I have done a thousand dreadful things
As willingly as one would kill a fly,
And nothing grieves me heartily indeed
But that I cannot do ten thousand more."
William Shakespeare - Titus Andronicus: Act 5, Scene 1

"Every villain is a hero in his own mind."
Tim Hiddleston, actor, on playing the character "Loki" in Marvel Comic movies.

"Nothing in his life
Became him like the leaving it"
William Shakespeare – Macbeth: Act 1, Scene 4

Chapter 1
Elaine
Saturday Night, July 5, 1952

Elaine Samuels grabbed the cold bottle of Narragansett beer that dripped with condensation, slapped a dollar on the bar and took a long swig. The bartender gave her a look and pushed the bill back.

"Thanks, Frankie."

He winked. "Professional courtesy."

"I can really use it tonight. I owe you one."

"Forget it." He smiled. "Tough night?"

Elaine nodded and took a sip. "Sometimes I get sick of smiling and wiggling my hips, but men give the tips and they like to look."

She had just finished her shift waitressing at the Mayflower Café, a restaurant and bar in Provincetown. The Mayflower was a town institution. It was her first summer working there and she loved the Janoplis family business that had been around since 1929. On the left wall were funny caricature drawings of famous people and local characters, drawn by Jake Spencer, a bar regular. Rumor had it that sometimes Mike Janoplis accepted the drawings to cover Jake's large bar tab.

It was a busy Saturday night on the steamy holiday weekend and Elaine was beat. With the windows and doors open, the salty smell of the harbor permeated the air. The night was so still you could hear the chatter of pedestrians and the sounds from the fish pier across the street. The Fourth of July was the official start of the Cape's summer season, and good news from an economic standpoint. Most Cape residents made the bulk of their income in the busy season, but it came with a price. It meant putting up with traffic, crowds and pushy city folks who wanted a vacation, but had not adjusted to a slower, more relaxing pace.

"One guy says to me what is that odor? Smells like rotten eggs," laughed Elaine. "I told him, welcome to fish guts and low tide at Provincetown Harbor."

Franky grinned, "I know, I think they want the movie version without the smell of fish processing and mud flats. Like a Hollywood film starring Spencer Tracy or Jimmy Stewart."

"Well, I ain't no Doris Day. They want America's Sweetheart, they should go to the cinema. My cheeks are so tired from faking a smile that I've got a headache."

To be fair, most of the tourists were nice, curious about the Cape, and full of questions for a native. However, some wanted the local residents to know how important they were, and seemed to feel the natives were one step above domesticated animals. One table of New York/New Jersey accents had given Elaine a particularly hard time. The women were whiny, and asked a million questions about how the seafood was prepared. The men made rude suggestive comments as their leering eyes stared at her chest.

"I had one table, man, if they weren't customers I would've punched them."

The oppressive heat of the day had seeped into the building, and she took a seat at the far end of the bar, close to one of the establishment's fans. Now she wanted to relax and have a few drinks before heading home to Bound Brook.

Provincetown was once a struggling Portuguese fishing community, but artists, writers and tourists had adopted the town. Its unique atmosphere, a blend of old-world charm and rugged seashore beauty, drew people from all corners of the earth. Elaine hadn't traveled far from the Cape, but she believed the people who said there was no other place quite like "P'town."

She knew most of the men in the bar. Fishermen and workmen, their clothes carried the odor of fish and sweat. They were regulars; some gave her a nod or a wink, but all of them gave her a long look through the smoky haze. No surprise, her tight black t-shirt and white shorts accentuated her curves. She pulled the bow from her ponytail so the long, black hair framed her striking Mediterranean features. At thirty-one Elaine was still a male magnet, although her face was just starting to show the signs of a hard life: too much booze and too many men.

She was used to the attention, part of life when you are pretty and have a good shape. In her younger years, it had been her treasure—the only thing that got her noticed and made her feel worth something. Now, it seemed a burden. Mostly it got her the wrong kind of attention and combined with her own recklessness often caused trouble.

"Hey, Elaine, you still need a lift home?"

She looked up at Arnold "Moose" Parker, the bar's custodian, doorman, bouncer and general handyman. Moose had been her classmate at Bound Brook High.

"Sure, Moose, that would be great."

He gave her a shy smile and went back to his station by the door. She shook her head. Moose was an imposing figure and had been the class bully, but around women, he was meek and tongue-tied. Maybe she should have latched on to him instead of the string of low-life losers that dotted her life.

She pulled a crushed pack of Pall Malls out of her back pocket and shook out a cigarette.

The small flame from a lighter appeared. "Allow me."

On her left was a handsome man. He seemed to be around her age, maybe a little younger, with classic, chiseled features, short haircut and dressed in a polo shirt, tan slacks and shiny shoes.

"This seat taken?"

"Nope! Free country, free seat."

"Well, it's my lucky night, an open seat at the bar next to the prettiest girl on the Cape."

Elaine rolled her eyes and gave him a smirk. "Boy, that's original. So what's your rank?"

"It's that obvious?"

"Buzz cut hair, neat clean civvies, and I've never seen you before . . . adds up to Camp Wellfleet. Also, the United States Army logo on your cigarette lighter was a pretty good clue."

He threw his head back and laughed. "Ok, you nailed it. I'm Ted, Ted Bowers, or Sergeant Bowers when I'm on the base. And you are?"

"Elaine Samuels, technically Elaine Stevens, but nobody, including me, calls me that."

"I sense that there's a longer story there."

"Actually, a very short story. Army guy, like you, near the end of the war, back from Germany. Another bar, another pick-up line, too much to drink and it was love at first sight. A week later, we were married and three days later he shipped out to God-knows-where. Never seen him since, and haven't missed him a bit." She took a long pull from her beer.

"Well, I feel it's my responsibility to compensate for the U.S. Army's dereliction of duty. Let me buy you something stronger than that Gansett."

Elaine waved to Frankie. "Rum and Coke, please."

"Gin and tonic," said Ted. "Put them on my tab."

Frankie nodded, but gave Bowers a frown.

"So, you got my story, what's yours, Sergeant Ted Bowers? Why did you join the army?"

"My father was army and he came from Mt. Carmel, Illinois. He named me for a Union Civil War hero who came from that town and had the same name. The combination sealed my fate; it was just assumed I'd join the army."

"Following in Daddy's footsteps?"

"I hope not. He was a jerk, drank too much and beat my mother. When I enlisted, it was either stay home and probably kill him or answer the call of Uncle Sam."

"Well, that gives us one thing in common: my parents were drunks."

"So, we probably should change the subject. Tell me about Cape Cod, and I'll tell you about some of the places I've been stationed that weren't in war zones."

*****

After the rum and Coke, Elaine switched to shots of bourbon while Ted nursed two more gin and tonics. Moose remembered Ted from the previous weekend. He'd been in Friday night, and walked around chatting with some of the guys. Then he'd gotten into a whispered conversation with Brian Francis, and the two of them had ducked out of the bar for ten minutes. Brian was not a nice guy, and not exactly the most law abiding. When they got back, Ted had chatted with Liz Santos and then later she had left with him. The next night Liz's father, Sal, had come in with murder in his eyes, looking for "that army guy." Fortunately, he wasn't there.

Moose gave Frankie a look, then moved his eyes to the couple at the bar. Frankie cocked his head and nodded, indicating that Moose should come over.

"You know that guy, Frankie?"

"Not really, but I don't trust him. I know Elaine can take care of herself, but I wish she'd ditch him."

Moose nodded, "I get this feeling about him, like I know something, but I can't put my finger on it."

Frankie leaned close and whispered, "Something happened with Liz Santos that made her old man mad as hell. Liz is a nice girl; I don't think she knows how to handle a guy like him. I wish Sal Santos had found him. I wouldn't want to mess with Sal when he's mad. If that guy did something to Liz, I'd give Sal a hand with the job."

"Wish I could remember where I've seen him before." Moose shook his head, but the memory didn't click. He went back to the door, where he focused his attention on Elaine and Ted.

The bar had started to empty. "Last call!" yelled Frankie.

Part of Elaine was kicking herself: *Here we go again, another pick-up. When am I ever gonna learn?* However, Ted seemed intelligent and he certainly was good looking. He had striking eyes, grey or light blue maybe; she couldn't tell in the dim light. He had a trim, athletic build and well-toned muscles stretched his short sleeve shirt.

"This muggy heat is brutal. I'm new here, is there some place we could go to cool off? You must know all the beaches."

Elaine paused. "Sure, what the hell. I know a spot: a nice, cool pond. Let's go."

Ted threw a bunch of bills on the bar and gave Frankie a nod.

Heading to the door, Elaine smiled at Moose. "I'm all set for a ride; thanks anyway. I'm gonna cool off my new friend in Bound Brook Pond."

"I can pick you up on my way home if you want."

Elaine gave him a tipsy giggle. "Maybe next time, old buddy."

"Alright." Moose glared at Ted. "Be careful ... both of you."

Ted winked. "Will do, big guy."

Out on Commercial Street, Elaine wobbled as they started down the sidewalk.

"Careful, kid." Ted took her arm. "Let me help; we've got to walk around the corner. It was so crowded I had to park on the backstreet."

They took a left on Standish to Bradford Street, where Ted had parked his army Jeep.

"I'm impressed; you get your own Jeep? Thought you were just a Sergeant."

"The Lieutenant is the only officer until tomorrow, and he is so green he needs me to tell him what to do. So, basically that leaves me in charge." He laughed. "Rank has its privileges, and you know Sergeants really run the army."

Bowers drove the road along the bay past rows of tourist cottages. A full moon reflected off the still water. In ten minutes, the road connected to the newly completed double-lane highway. A few minutes later, Elaine pointed to a road off the highway to the left. A bit over a mile down the twisty back road, she pointed left again and the Jeep turned down a rutted, dirt road with over-hanging branches that ended in a small parking lot overlooking a circular body of water twinkling in the moonlight. The outline of a small raft broke the mirror glass reflection.

Elaine leaped out of the open Jeep and ran down the slope. "Last one in's a rotten egg!"

Ted followed a trail of sneakers, shorts, and t-shirt as he heard a splash and then a screech. "Wow, that's cold."

He smiled as he removed his loafers, slacks and polo shirt. He waded up to his knees, took a deep breath and dove forward.

*****

Moose nodded to the last customer and locked the door. He looked at Frankie, who was washing the last of the glasses.

"Frankie, it just dawned on me, I think I know who that guy is, and if I'm right Elaine could be in trouble. Would you mind if I split out of here? I'm gonna take a ride to Bound Brook Pond."

"Think that might be a good idea. I'll sweep up for you."

"Thanks."

"Moose, you think you need to take that with you?" Frankie pointed toward the baseball bat he kept behind the bar for protection.

"No, I'm sure I can handle things myself."

Moose hurried out the door, climbed in the old Chevy pick-up he had parked in the alley, cut through a driveway and came out on Bradford. The P'town police cruiser was parked in the gas station on the corner, and he waved to Tony Oliver who was waiting to pull over any drunks. Once he got past Tony, he picked up speed. Probably no other cops were out this late, and he had a sense of urgency.

Moose made good time on the empty highway, turned left on the paved back road and pulled the old pick-up onto the dirt road to the pond. He slowed down to try to minimize the truck's noisy bouncing, then put in the clutch and coasted alongside an army Jeep. With the engine off, he could hear splashing, voices and laughter. Then the laughter changed to anger.

"I told you NO, not here, not NOW!"

More muffled voices, then a deep voice, "DAMN, that hurt. I'll get you for that, bitch!"

Moose jumped out of the truck, ran down the slope and bumped into Elaine. The shadow of Ted was splashing out of the water with mumbled curses.

"Get in my truck."

"I'll just grab my clothes."

Ted squinted at the large form moving toward the water's edge. "She bit my hand. I'll probably need a tetanus shot. Look." Bowers stepped closer, holding out his hand as evidence.

Moose lunged, at the same time thrusting both arms forward. The heels of his hands hit Bowers in the solar plexus, the force driving him backward, where he sprawled in the shallow water.

"Stay away from Elaine! And I better not see you in the Mayflower again. You hear me?"

The only sound was Bowers gasping for breath.

Moose climbed the slope and found Elaine in the truck, dripping wet, but dressed in her shorts and t-shirt. "You alright?"

"Yeah, I'm fine. That jerk started getting rough."

"I'm taking you home."

"Thank God you got here, Moose."

He could feel himself blushing, as he mumbled, "No sweat."

Then the two were quiet as the pick-up bumped down the road and out to the highway. They only passed two other sets of headlights on the ride back to Bound Brook.

"Moose, would you mind staying with me tonight? I don't want to be alone. I just need to know someone is there."

"Sure, Elaine, I'll take care of you."

*****

Bowers stretched back in the shallow water and tried to stay calm. He'd had the wind knocked out of him before, and his brain told him he would be all right, while his body panicked without any air. Then a breath, a big intake of air, rushed to fill his lungs. In a few minutes, his breathing became steady.

Between the drinks and his lack of oxygen, Ted felt drained. He let the cool water lap over his body. His right hand now started to throb. With his left-hand fingers, he felt a ridge where Elaine's teeth had found their target. The fresh liquid was soothing and he let himself relax. It would be easy to stay in the comforting pond. Despite the pain, he felt at peace. Maybe he could stay here floating in the calming fluid. Time slipped by.

His brain started to clear, and he realized his night was done. He might as well head back to the Camp. He had pressured the Lieutenant into giving him the night off. The poor kid was so new he needed Bowers to tell him what to do. So he had headed into Provincetown for the night: part business with Brian Francis and, he had hoped, part pleasure. With the new base commander and supporting team of officers due tomorrow afternoon, it might be his last chance for the rest of the summer.

Ted pulled himself up, stood calf deep in the pond and took a deep breath. A noise caught his attention. "Someone there?" A shadow came down the slope.

"Not you again? Okay, you made your point; I'll leave her alone, nothing happened anyway."

The shadow moved closer and he saw a slim figure, not Moose's bulky form. Then came recognition.

"Oh, I know you. What are you doing here?"

The figure stepped closer, one foot in the pond, a long arm raised high above its head. Bewildered, Ted couldn't comprehend how the arm could be so long. Too late he understood. The arm swung down, and some kind of club smashed into his shoulder. He screamed in pain as he heard a bone crack.

"What the hell are you doing?"

The long arm pulled back in a circular arc that ended with the club crashing down on Ted's skull. The last thing he heard was, "You shall reap what you sow."

Chapter 2
Jimmy
Monday, June 30, 1952 (five days earlier)

He had never remembered his dreams. Of course, he knew he had dreamed and as he awoke, the soft details hovered on the fringe of his consciousness. Before he was fully awake, he could see the flicker of images. When he opened his eyes and came back to reality the scenes were gone. Maybe his rational mind couldn't deal with the irrational jumble of his dreams. Then, war had changed all that.

Now every incoherent detail flamed and burned. War and dreams were alike; neither made any sense. The action of battle was all emotion, heightened senses, instant reactions and constant numbing terror. The insanity of battles made dreams seem sane. Now he remembered every detail. It was easy because the dream was always the same.

They walked right into it. Exhausted troops pushing forward, following unrealistic orders. Command seemed to forget there was a dangerous enemy, harsh terrain and brutal thirty-degree-below-zero temperatures between them and their goal. The scuttlebutt was that if they could get past the Chosin Reservoir and to the Chinese border at the Yalu River, they would be home by Christmas.

He felt it again, that tingling. Despite the brutal cold, he broke out in a sweat. It was a sixth sense from years of combat in two wars. It just didn't feel right. He raised his hand for the unit to halt, but then they came: A horde of white clad Chinese barely visible against the snow. Beside him, Corporal Johnson went down. He opened fire, but they were everywhere. Then his own men were running. He tried to stop them, but they ran

right past him. Bowled over, he was trampled by thousands of
Chinese. He struggled to get to his feet, but it was useless.

Then the scene changed and they were assaulting a
ridgeline with the enemy above them. The snow was gone and
the weather was crisp, but not freezing. His men were hardened
veterans now and they moved with confidence and efficiency.
This objective was critical, but Christmas 1950 was almost a
year ago and they had never made it home for the holiday.
Then he was confused about which ridge they were attacking:
was it the one they called Bloody Ridge or the one dubbed
Heart Break? They all blurred together.

Again, he felt the eerie tingling and again he raised his
hand, but his men didn't stop. He tried to yell a warning but
nothing came out. He watched helplessly as the Chinese surged
toward them. His men walked forward, smiling and without a
care. Rifle fire picked them off one at a time. Some turned and
waved to him before they fell. Then all the men were gone and
he was alone. Hundreds of rifles opened fire, all of them aimed
at him. Something stung his hand. He fired as fast as possible,
but the enemy kept coming. An Asian face gave him a hideous
smile as a hand threw a grenade. His legs collapsed under him
before he flew through the air and then it all went black. A
voice said, "Now you might get home for Christmas."

Thrashing and kicking, he threw the covers aside and
sat up with a jolt. A deep gasp and then he was awake. The
same dream. It never ended well.

*****

James Curtis adjusted his crisp, white, short-sleeve
shirt. He hooked his fingers along the side seams and pulled the
front tight and wrinkle free. He felt the scars from the shrapnel
like hard ridges along his left side. It was awkward, but he had

learned to adjust to the missing fingers on his left hand. He hitched up his slacks, zippered, buttoned and then adjusted his belt. The buttons of the shirt lined up perfectly with the end of his buckle and the line of his zipper, all three forming a straight line. The habits from years in the military didn't end just because he was a civilian, and like in the army, he had been awake since dawn.

"Jimmy," called his mother, Mabel.

"Be right there."

"Got oatmeal, eggs, toast and coffee ready. Don't want to make you late."

"I've got plenty of time."

Thirty-one-years old, and living with his mother once again. He had to chuckle. Two wars, enemy fire, sleeping on the ground in freezing weather, babysitting green teenagers, and here he was home in Bound Brook, Cape Cod, with his mother clucking over him like a hen. He hated to admit it, but it felt pretty darn good.

He took his time over breakfast while his mother bustled around the kitchen, obviously pleased to have him home. Jim hadn't planned on coming back to Bound Brook; in fact, it had been the last place he wanted to be. Bound Brook represented a failed marriage, guilty feelings, and too much liquor. He had hoped to stay in the army and make it his career. Sergeant First Class Curtis was an exceptional soldier and loved the order, discipline and adrenaline rush of warfare. It was ironic that his last combat had earned him two more medals, and yet was his ticket out of the army.

Mabel Curtis sat down across from her son, reached out and placed her hand on top of his. "I know you're disappointed, but I am so relieved to have you home. Every day I dreaded that I would get bad news. When I heard you were wounded . . . at first, I feared the worst. You know, you're all I have left."

She patted his hand, got up and turned away, dabbing the mist from her eyes.

"It's okay, Mom." He smiled. "I guess you're stuck with me."

Jimmy's father, Charlie Curtis, had been in the merchant marine. He had made a good living, but frequent long trips were part of the deal: extended time at home followed by months at sea. The last voyage had been Jimmy's senior year, before the U.S. had officially entered the war. In November of 1939, his father had been engineering chief on a cargo ship headed to England with much needed supplies. They had been part of a convoy, but a storm had scattered the ships, and in submarine-infested waters, his ship had never been found. Had it sunk in the storm, or had a German U-boat sent it to the bottom, determined to prevent its supplies from getting to Great Britain?

It bothered him that his father's name would never be on the War Memorial in front of the Town Hall. It wouldn't bring him back, but it would have been nice to see him honored. However, the United States hadn't been at war yet, so Charles Curtis was just a name on a headstone in Pine Grove Cemetery. He was one of many Bound Brook sailors with empty graves who had been lost at sea. Like the minister had said at his father's funeral:

"They that go down to the sea in ships, that do business in great waters;
These see the works of the Lord, and his wonders in the deep."

Jimmy had never been religious. Well sure, he'd gone to the Methodist church because Mabel made him, but it was just a routine with no real meaning. Of course, the overzealous preaching of Reverend Duggan had been entertaining, and his righteous ranting kept you awake. It was in the freezing forests of the Battle of the Bulge during World War II, and then again in the freezing mountains of Korea, that the words of his church years had come back to his mind. It reminded him of the quote, "There are no atheists in foxholes." When you're trapped in a foxhole, you try to touch all the bases.

He felt himself pulled back into that black mood that haunted his dreams and made him a changed man. It had turned Bound Brook from his beloved hometown, full of fond memories of friendships and basketball teammates, into the place that brought out the worst in him, making him a mean, surly and ungrateful man who drowned his anger in a bottle.

"Let me warm up your coffee."

Jim snapped back to reality. "Thanks, Mom."

"It was nice of George to arrange this job for you. I know it's only for the summer, but it'll be something to do while you find more permanent work."

George Gilmore had been his high school teacher, principal and basketball coach, and he was also Jim's father-in-law, at least for now. Gilmore worked at the new PX at Camp Wellfleet, and had gotten him a job there as well. Today would be Jim's first day at work in the nearby town. Camp Wellfleet had been an active military base during World War II. The previous year, the army had decided to reopen it and this summer the base continued construction while bringing in National Guard units for their annual two weeks of summer military training. The Guard units would have to live in pup tents, while a small regular army detachment and civilian construction workers built barracks, roads and observation towers for what would become the largest anti-aircraft training facility in the country.

Jim finished the last of his breakfast, gulped his black coffee, and stood up from the table.

"You sure you don't need the car today, Mom?"

"No, I'm fine; I went to the A&P on Saturday and stocked up. Made a couple of baloney and cheese sandwiches for you. They're on the counter."

"I'm going to stop at Hooper's Flying A on the way home, and see if they know about a used car I can buy. I've got enough back pay to get something decent."

He kissed his mother on the cheek and went out the door to her car. The seat was too far forward, and he had some trouble bending his stiff left knee as he squeezed behind the wheel. Adjusting the seat, he backed out of the driveway. *Well, here I go*, he thought. *Welcome back to civilian life.*

Jim shifted the 1948 Chrysler Coupe and headed down Curtis Lane to Herring Brook Road. The thick shrubbery was in full bloom and almost blocked the view of the meandering Herring Brook. He remembered roaming through the marsh and woods with his friends Rob Caldwell and Horace "Hoopy" Hooper when they were about 12 years old. The Three Musketeers were their heroes and the trio of friends would spend the day tromping through the pine trees, isolated groves of cedar, shrubs and cat-of-nine-tails. Hoopy had a target bow with a dozen arrows; Jimmy had a BB gun; all three had sharpened wooden swords. It had been a magical time of life. As the Three Musketeers, King Arthur with Lancelot and Gawain, or Billy the Kid with Frank and Jesse James, the trio roamed the back woods of Bound Brook. Their enemies were wild Indians or French knights. They hunted squirrels, rabbits, foxes or the herring in the brook. Arrows had flown and BBs were shot, but the animals and fish had usually escaped unscathed.

In eighth grade, the trio had welcomed another member, the new girl in school, Rachel Gilmore. Rachel was the only child of George Gilmore, the new teaching principal and basketball coach of Bound Brook Consolidated School. Redheaded Rachel was a tomboy, who had no trouble keeping up with three boys. Soon they were regulars at the Gilmore house on Tyler Hill. All three of them had adolescent crushes on the pretty and vivacious girl, but it was obvious that Rob and Rachel had a special bond. Rob was an amazing athlete, the star of Bound Brook's championship basketball team, with Jimmy and Hoopy also playing key roles. Rob and Rachel were boyfriend and girlfriend all through high school, until a drunken tryst between Rob and Elaine Samuels had led to a break-up. In a rebound reaction, Rachel had turned to Jimmy, and impulsively the two had eloped. It was ill fated from the start and both had paid the price for years. Now they were in a mutually agreed process of divorce, and Rob and Rachel had renewed a relationship that never should have ended.

Jimmy sighed, *Strange how marrying the girl of my dreams has ruined my life.* It wasn't Rachel's fault. Despite his poor treatment, she had been loyal for years. However, it had consumed him with guilt. He had stolen his best friend's girlfriend when she was at a weak moment. He had known Rachel cared for him, but didn't truly love him.

In his guilt, he had turned to the bottle, and his anger at himself had made him surly and rude. His former friends had avoided him, for good reason. When he had joined the army, nobody knew or cared about his past. The discipline and excitement had given him structure and a sense of self-worth. He had found that he was a really good soldier.

Herring Brook Road now took him out to the newly completed Route 6 highway that led him into Wellfleet, the location of the base. The Chrysler purred smoothly down Route 6, past the South Wellfleet General Store and past Blackfish Creek. He took the left at the entrance to Camp Wellfleet and stopped at the guard station. A uniformed private with a clipboard stepped out of the guard shack.

"Sir, what is the purpose of your visit?"

"I'm starting work today at the PX."

He handed Jim the clipboard. "Please fill in your name and address."

He took back the clipboard, recorded the car's plate number and then waved him through. Jimmy was back on an army base, but for the first time in two years, he was a civilian.

Chapter 3
George
Monday Morning

George Gilmore stood near the door of the Camp Wellfleet Post Exchange (PX), and watched the store's manager, Simon Eldredge, rummaging through the stacks of boxes randomly scattered around the building. Two weeks ago, workers had finished the basic structure: a wood-framed metal building, common on military bases. Sometimes called Quonset huts, they were easy to assemble and quick to take down. As soon as the building was finished and there were locks on the doors, trucks started delivering loads of cartons for the store's inventory. George had started work the week before and was already impatient with Eldredge.

George spread out the diagram of the store layout on top of two cardboard boxes. The PX was a civilian enterprise that had a contract to provide store services to the soldiers confined to their base. All the Post Exchanges used a standard layout. The only adjustment was to adapt the design to the size of the store. Camp Wellfleet's PX was slightly larger than a school classroom, maybe half-again that size. (As a teacher, George often used education as his base of reference.)

Long cardboard boxes were stacked along the back wall, containing metal shelving units ready for assembly. The diagram showed where to organize them into the store's retail departments. George suggested to Simon that they open those boxes and start to assemble the shelves, and then move the product boxes to the sections of the store that matched the products: jewelry-to-jewelry, cigarettes-to-cigarettes. This seemed so simple and logical that George tried to say it routinely, so it didn't sound too critical.

Simon glared at him. "I'm the manager. I'll decide how it's done."

That had been on Monday, a week ago. In the meantime, Simon had George sweeping the floor, which would soon be covered again with the debris from a hundred boxes, and waiting for the remaining shipments of the last of the inventory. Simon fluttered around, trying to look busy and important, muttering to himself as if he had had a revelation, and then pointing out areas of the floor George had missed with the broom. It was going to be a long summer, if he could last that long.

The good news was that as the week dragged on Simon spent less time in the store. He started to disappear on "important errands." George took the initiative and managed to get things accomplished while Eldredge was away. Although he was in his mid-fifties, the former three-sport athlete was in good shape. He moved the shelving boxes to one location, pulling all the boxes away from the walls where shelves had to be mounted. He opened boxes, pulled out their contents lists, and organized them into their product locations.

When Simon returned he had looked around with a scowl, and asked George what he had done. When George told him, Simon cut him off. "Well, I would've expected you could've gotten more done. You had plenty of time." Of course, this was ridiculous, since Simon hadn't given George any directions except to sweep.

Today, George hoped to make some progress. Both Jim Curtis, back from the war, and Benny Brown, just graduated from Bound Brook High, were starting full-time.

At first, Simon had insisted on having the only key to the PX, but that had changed on Tuesday when Simon left before the end of the workday on another "important" errand. George reminded him that he would need to lock up the store.

Simon frowned and handed him an extra key, looking at it as if it unlocked the treasure of Fort Knox.

Taking advantage of the opportunity, George now arrived each morning at seven-thirty and managed to get work accomplished before Eldredge came in, sometime around nine o'clock. What was even more frustrating was that Simon's disorganized puttering frequently moved the boxes George had organized into a logical system, putting them back into random disorder. George was starting to feel he was shoveling against the tide.

He had called Jimmy and Benny the night before, and asked them to do him a favor and show up for work fifteen or twenty minutes before the nine o'clock starting time, so he could give them directions and get them going before Simon arrived. Then, lo and behold, Simon had inexplicably shown up at eight-thirty.

Now he was on a manic mission, tossing boxes about randomly, ripping them open and searching for God-only-knew-what. Simon paused over one box and peered inside, then pulled package stuffing that went flying in every direction. He reached into the box, removed an object and let out a squeak of delight, then gave George a furtive look and stuffed the object in his pocket.

George heard voices and saw the two new helpers walking toward the building. They came through the door and he shook hands with Jim and Benny. "Let me introduce you to our boss. Simon, this is Jim Curtis and Benny Brown, our new workers."

Simon looked at the pair suspiciously. "Don't do anything unless I tell you to. Never forget who is in charge here." With that, he just walked out the door. Then, over his shoulder, "George, make sure you get work done. I won't permit any loafing or goofing off."

Jim and Benny just looked at George with perplexed expressions. "What was that all about?" asked Benny.

"If we can't do anything unless he tells us to, and he doesn't tell us anything to do, then what are we supposed to do?" said Jim.

All George could do was laugh. "Sad to say, but Simon is clueless and helpless. He wants to be important, but he has no idea what to do or how to do it. Just make him feel important, and then we'll do what needs to be done.

"Here, let me show you the layout. First thing we need to do is assemble all these shelving units. Over there are the boxes with the pliers, wrenches and tools they shipped us. If you open any boxes, make sure you keep the packing slips."

For the next three hours, they assembled the racks for the inventory displays and placed them in the designated locations. Simon came in once, looked around with a frown, went over to one of the shelving units, gave it a shake and said, "This one's loose, tighten it up." Then he was gone.

"Seems like we are going to spend the summer playing a game of *Simon Says*," quipped Jim.

"We better do what *Simon Says*," laughed Benny. "*Simon says*—tighten that up."

Chapter 4
Rob
Monday, 9:30 a.m.

Sipping his morning coffee, Rob Caldwell reread the article in yesterday's Sunday edition of the *Cape Cod Standard Times*. "Hero Returns Home," screamed the headline. It seemed odd to be reading about his old friend from childhood.

Sergeant First Class James Curtis, a native of Bound Brook, returned home last week from service in Korea. Curtis has recovered from injuries that led to him receiving the Purple Heart for his combat wounds and the Silver Star for his heroic action under fire. The Silver Star citation states:

"Sergeant First Class James Curtis performed exemplary service throughout his tour in Korea. At Heart Break Ridge in an engagement with a numerically superior force, Sergeant First Class Curtis provided covering fire that stopped the enemy counter attack and allowed his platoon to withdraw to a safer area. Curtis was wounded in the initial assault, but held his position until other wounded men were evacuated. Curtis continued firing at the enemy, inflicting numerous casualties, as he withdrew to join his men.

"When his Lieutenant received fatal wounds, Curtis assumed command of the platoon. He directed his men into a defensive perimeter that succeeded in halting the enemy advance and continued to lead his platoon despite additional wounds from an enemy grenade. His leadership and courage contributed to a decisive victory. For courageous action in the face of enemy fire,

Sergeant First Class James Curtis is awarded the Silver Star for valor and the Purple Heart for his combat wounds."
Curtis, a veteran of World War II, parachuted into France on D-Day and fought in the Battle of the Bulge and the invasion of Germany. For his heroic service in WWII Curtis received a Bronze Star with V for valor. Curtis plans to return to civilian life and is unsure of his future career plans. Certainly, his heroic actions and military service should make him a much sought-after candidate by numerous employers. Cape Cod extends its Thank You to James Curtis for his service to his country in two wars and welcomes him back to his home peninsula.

Rob felt a rush of mixed emotions: relief that Jimmy was home and safe after a narrow escape in Korea, but concerned for the future of his once best friend. Now, Jimmy and his wife, Rachel Gilmore Curtis, were in the process of a divorce, and Rob and Rachel had renewed their romance after a twelve-year break. Jimmy loved the army and didn't have a very good civilian history, so Rob hoped he could make the adjustment.

Rachel had just finished the first semester at Boston University's summer session. The college required the summer session for adults who had been out of school for several years. If she did well, they would accept her for the fall semester as a fully matriculated student. She had aced her classes.

Rob wasn't surprised that she had breezed through the two introductory classes in college English and math; Rachel was smart and had been a top student in high school. She had stayed with her uncle and aunt in Winchester during the week, taking the train into Boston each day for her courses. Her schedule had given her a long weekend with no classes on Friday, so Rob had met her at the train station in Yarmouth on Thursday nights. Although Rachel now lived with her parents, it had given them the weekend together to start making up for all the lost years.

The crunch of tires on his crushed-shell driveway announced Rachel's arrival. She pulled up in a 1938 DeSoto sedan and parked next to his almost-new '51 Chevy pick-up truck.

"Got any coffee left?"

He stood in the doorway as auburn-haired Rachel got out of the old jalopy, thinking once again, *Wow, is she beautiful!* In jean shorts, a checkered short-sleeve blouse and white canvas low-top sneakers, Rachel looked like a magazine ad for the All-American girl.

"Only if you've been taking good care of my old DeSoto."

Rachel laughed. "You mean *my* DeSoto? Remember you sold it to me?"

"How can I forget after your tough negotiation?"

"You are a jerk!" She gave him a poke in the ribs. "You're the one that sold it to me for a dollar. I tried to give you more."

"Like I said, it was tough negotiating for me to hold you down to a buck, and don't I get more than a punch?"

"Bend down."

Rob bent his six-foot-three-inch frame, to get a peck on his cheek. "You can do better than that." He wrapped his arms around her in an embrace that pulled her off the ground. They beamed at each other before locking into a deep kiss. Finally, they eased away and he lowered her to the ground.

"Wow, I like that greeting better than the wisecracks. Maybe you better get that coffee before this gets too carried away."

"Yes ma'am, have a seat. Coffee coming right up."

*****

Rachel looked around the small cottage as Rob filled the percolator with coffee and water. She sat at the kitchen table, just big enough for four chairs, and admired the collection of artwork on the knotty pine walls. His mother, Roberta, had painted the seascapes, landscapes and ships, as well as handcrafting the wool hooked-rugs that covered the rough floorboards. One room, a combination kitchen, dining area and living room with a tiny bedroom off the back, was all that comprised the bayside cabin. It had been Rob's home before the accident that had claimed his mother's life when he was just thirteen. He reclaimed the rustic cottage after he returned to Bound Brook following the war and college.

"So tell me about your plans to fix it up," she began.

"Well, I'm turning the back bedroom into a hallway that will connect to two bedrooms, with a bathroom in between."

"So, after all these years, you have running water and a flush toilet? You even got a telephone installed last week. Guess we don't have to communicate by smoke signals anymore."

"Yes sirree, joining the modern age. Ben is going to do the rest of the plumbing once the new walls and roof are finished. Right now I've just got an outside shower."

Ben Brown was Rob's cousin by marriage, but he had been more like his foster father. He and his wife, Phyllis Tyler Brown, Rob's cousin, raised him after his mother's death. Rob was part of the extended Tyler clan, and was protected and nurtured by the entire web of cousins and in-laws, most of whom lived in the area of town known as Tyler's Tangle.

"Running water, indoor plumbing . . . What about electricity and heat?"

"Electric company is running the lines from the highway, and we'll hook it up when the house is done. Jimmy Wilkinson from Wellfleet is doing the wiring." Rob paused. "Still not decided about the type of heating system, but I know the wood stove won't be able to heat the whole house. I got the lumber delivery from BCL a few days ago, and been digging a new foundation hole for the extension."

Rachel glanced at the Sunday paper. "Been reading about Jimmy?"

"Yes, have you talked with him since he's been back?"

She nodded. "I went over to Mabel's and ran into him. We mostly talked about the divorce paperwork. He looks good, lost a couple of fingers and his leg is stiff and will give him a permanent limp, but otherwise he looks the same. No, actually, he looks healthier than when he left. The drinking was taking its toll on him. Have you seen him?"

"Not yet. I've been focused on getting the cottage project off the ground, and told Chief Foster I need to cut back on my special police duties after the 4th of July if he can spare me."

"My father got Jimmy a job at the new PX at Camp Wellfleet, think he started work today. You know it probably would be good if the two of you had a talk."

"I'm sure I'll run into him; town this size it's inevitable. Here's your coffee. Milk and two lumps, right?"

Rachel frowned. "Sure, you two have put off talking for twelve years. What's another year or two, right?"

He shrugged. "What's to say?"

"I give up, I'll drop the subject." Rachel took the steaming mug. "Let's sit outside?" She went out the door, sat in one of the four collapsible beach chairs lined along the west side of the cottage and gazed at the view.

It was half-tide with the bay flowing out. Seagulls squawked as they swooped near the exposed mudflats. Two gulls engaged in a brief spat as they fought over some flotsam. A pickup truck bounced past the driveway, no doubt bound for the shellfish beds at nearby Cove Beach. It looked like one of the Tyler clan heading off to tend to his oyster grant. Rob joined her, sipping from his mug of black coffee.

"Spending time in Boston, does it ever make you feel like leaving the Cape?"

She smiled. "The city is exciting; there's always something going on, lots of hustle and bustle, some good and some bad. It's fun to go in each day, but then it's nice to leave it and go back to my uncle's place in Winchester. But no, the best part of the week is coming home to the Cape each weekend. It's been nice getting to know my Uncle Arthur and Aunt Laura better, and they're good company . . . But I kinda like the company of a certain eligible bachelor in Bound Brook.

"What about you? You have an Ivy League degree, lots of experience, you worked in France and speak the language. Don't you ever think you should be doing more with your life?"

He looked confused. "Like what?"

"I don't know. Sometimes you are dense, but this town thinks you are God's gift; you could be elected selectman in a heartbeat. Every female over twelve has a crush on you, and the men all wish they were you. You could run any business in this town, and if you tried, you could get job offers in Boston, Providence or New York City. But, here you sit, directing traffic and renovating your cottage. Do you have any plans?"

"Wow, where did this come from? A minute ago you said you were content to stay in Bound Brook. Now you're talking like someone with a lot more ambition."

"I know. I'm sorry. It's just that for twelve years, I was marking time being married to Jimmy, just stuck in a rut. All my dreams and hopes were on hold. Now, so much is in my mind . . . Well, it has me confused. I want to get a college degree and do something with my life, but I also want to stay in Bound Brook . . . And most of all I want you. I guess I want it all, and I don't want to wait."

Rob reached over and took her hand. "It must be a lot for you to deal with: divorce, us, college — and at your age."

"Excuse me, mister, let's be careful about the age comments."

He laughed. "You know what I mean."

"Yes, I do. I need to takes things one at a time. I can't get twelve years back, but I can make a new start, or maybe *we* can make one."

Chapter 5
Ted
Monday, Ten Hundred Hours

Sergeant Theodore Bowers had just finished his inspection of the platoon's morning duties. In two weeks, the first wave of one thousand Army National Guard Reservists would be streaming into Camp Wellfleet, and it was his platoon's job to make the site ready for them. It was not as hard as it sounded. His men had been preparing the grounds for the last month, with the help of some local contractors and their heavy equipment. The Guard units would have their own officers and non-coms, sergeants and corporals, with his platoon shoved to the back burner. That would fit perfectly into his plans.

The new troops would immediately start erecting two-man tents. They would simulate setting up a combat post "on-the–fly," just as if they had moved to a new position in a war zone. Of course, Bowers knew, and all too well, that in combat nobody would have raked the ground and created roads ahead of their arrival. Bowers' platoon had been helping to smooth the sandy grounds and prepare crude dirt/clay roads. Eventually all the road areas would be paved, but right now only the main one and the parking lots of the few completed buildings had the shiny black of new tar.

The only completed buildings were one enlisted barracks, with a section for NCOs, an Officers' Quarters, HQ command offices and the recently completed PX. A large tent served as the temporary enlisted mess hall. For now, the platoon needed to rely on local vendors to supply fresh food to supplement the army K-rations and packaged foods. When the National Guard arrived Bowers' men would move to a new area and continue to help with permanent buildings: multiple barracks, Officers' Quarters (and Club), NCO Club, church, mess halls, observation towers and more. The local civilian contractors had done the real work, under the direction of the Army Corps of Engineers. Bowers' platoon would handle base security, guard duty and whatever miscellaneous duties were required.

Ted Bowers had a love-hate relationship with the United States Army. He loved combat action and its thrilling rush. He reveled in making quick decisions and giving orders to his men. He tolerated officers because he had to, although he had to admit there had been a few lieutenants and captains who weren't completely worthless. The incompetent ones he had learned to "yessir" repeatedly, and then modify their orders just enough to keep himself and his men from being killed too easily.

Ted had joined the army at the end of 1943, soon after he turned eighteen. He had completed basic training in time to join the push through France and into Germany. He had risen through the ranks, earning battlefield promotions to corporal and sergeant, due to a combination of his skill and the attrition from the deaths and wounds of the NCOs.

He was a survivor, with the uncanny knack of a hunter and craftiness of an animal. He knew how and when to attack and he seemed to have a sixth sense about avoiding danger. Officers learned to trust Sergeant Bowers' instincts. When the war ended, his distinguished service, including a Bronze Star, had kept him in the army when most men were discharged. He also learned about a strange coincidence that only the army bureaucracy could screw up.

The original Theodore Bowers was a Civil War hero who had been a newspaper editor from Mt. Carmel, Illinois. He had risen to the rank of Brevet Brigadier General and been the personal aide to General, and then President, Ulysses S. Grant. General Bowers had died with no children and Ted was pretty sure his family was not related, but by a weird circumstance, his father had moved them to Mt. Carmel.

Knowing his father, Ted wasn't even sure if Bowers was their real last name. It wouldn't have surprised him if he had used a false identity. Anyway, he had named his only son Theodore, and people from the area just assumed there was a connection. Ted had encouraged the impression and learned the personal history of his "Great Uncle Ted."

When he enlisted in the army, someone had put a note in his file that he was from a distinguished military family. Once something gets in your file, right or wrong, it stays with you throughout your army career. It had been a fortunate error for Ted, because peacetime didn't provide him with enough adventure, so he had pushed the boundaries of army rules.

Most of the time he had gotten away with running scams, and over the years he had become a master at manipulating the army, to run his own small-time criminal enterprises. Honestly, it wasn't the money, which wasn't really that much; it was the thrill and the risk that made the boring life on an army base tolerable.

Throughout his nine-year career, Ted was busted in rank several times. The first time, he had to accept a move back to corporal at the end of the war. It was part of the conditions for him staying enlisted. The army needed fewer sergeants, not more. It hadn't taken long for him to work his way back to Sergeant, though.

Then he ran afoul with a captain, a West Pointer who couldn't stand Ted's callous disregard for rigid protocol. Later, a lieutenant almost discovered one of the side hustles. In both cases, he escaped with a temporary reduction in rank, but the note in his file about his distinguished military ancestor kept him from a discharge.

Then Communist North Korea invaded South Korea and Ted was off to war again. With his experience, he rose in rank to Sergeant First Class and earned another Bronze Star for heroic action during the brutal fighting. Then he had a problem with two other Sergeants and once again was busted back one rank and pay grade to regular Sergeant. Worse, somebody decided he needed to get out of Korea. He had gotten his revenge on one of the Sergeants. The other had been seriously wounded at Heartbreak Ridge, and Ted figured he'd never see him again.

He remembered his meeting with the company major. "Sergeant Bowers, it seems to me this isn't the first complaint you've had about your off-post behavior, is it?"

"No sir, there've been a few misunderstandings."

"Bowers, I know you. We were at Fort Benning together before this war. You are a helluva fighter. I'd take you as a combat sergeant any day. However, you seem to have problems whenever you are in civilian company too long. In my opinion you should be busted one grade, docked a month's pay, and sent back to the front where you can do the most good."

"Yes, sir, I guess that would be fair."

"Well, that's not what's going to happen, Sergeant. The army works in mysterious ways. Seems somebody put a special note in your personnel jacket and you get priority treatment. Unfortunately, that means you only get the pay grade demotion from Sergeant First Class to Sergeant. And here's the dumb part: you get shipped back home. I think the army is just asking for trouble, but the decision is from above me. So Sergeant, pack your bags, you're going back to the U.S. of A. And heaven help the sorry post that gets you, but at least you are not my problem anymore."

So, here he was in a backwater fishing village, shoveling sand and waiting for a bunch of weekend-warrior National Guard Troops. However, it wasn't all bad. Plenty of good-looking women from the small towns thought an army sergeant was glamorous. However, the best thing was the new base was built from scratch. Ted had specialized in steering some of the army goods and supplies to other places; some called it the black market. He had already stashed some construction materials in the thick brush of the marsh on the edge of the base. Now, by a fluke of army bureaucracy Ted had a rare opportunity. It was a classic army "SNAFU."

Second Lieutenant Gallant had briefed him on Thursday. "Sergeant, I had a meeting with the XO, and we have a situation. As you know, we are supposed to have the change of command ceremony tomorrow. Well, somebody screwed up. All the officers except me are scheduled to ship out late Friday, but the replacement officers won't be here for a week. Major Vance said that Lt. Colonel Flynn tried to get it changed, but no such luck. The Colonel, Major and Captain leave tomorrow, which leaves me in charge for a week until the new base commander and staff officers arrive."

Gallant was fresh out of college and ninety days in Officer Candidate School. In short, he was green as grass and looked nervous as hell.

"Lieutenant, you can count on me, sir."

Gallant swallowed hard, "Well yes, Sergeant, I know I can. It's only a week and we just have the platoon to worry about."

It had given Bowers a thought. On Friday, Gallant and Bowers marched the platoon to the HQ parking lot. Spit polished and in their dress uniforms, the men stood at attention for their final review by Lt. Colonel Flynn and the XO, Major Vance. Then Flynn, Vance and Captain Evans climbed into Jeeps, headed for flights to their next posts. Lieutenant Gallant dismissed the men and Ted saw his chance.

"Sir, may I make a suggestion?"

"By all means, Sergeant."

"I know the Captain handled interactions in town with food vendors and errands for the Colonel. I suggest that for the next week we both have authorization to use army transport to travel off base as needed. You're going to have your hands full and I can help."

The Lieutenant looked nervous. He glanced at the three hash marks on the Sergeant's sleeve that marked at least nine years' experience.

"Before you arrived," Bowers lied, "the Captain had that arrangement with me. That way I don't need to find you every time something is required off base."

"Well, I guess if the Captain did it, I can authorize it, but remember, it's just for this week while we're shorthanded."

Ted smiled to himself now as he remembered the conversation. Continuing his rounds, he approached the guard shack at the entrance to the base. When the pimply faced PFC saw Bowers, he snapped to attention.

"Any unusual visitors, Private?"

"No, Sergeant. Just the civilians who are on the list."

"Let me see that list, Private."

"Yes, Sergeant."

Bowers scanned the familiar list that included the civilian contractors and laborers, as well as two civilians who were setting up the new PX. Near the bottom of the list his eyes stopped.

"Private, who are these two new names?"

"Sergeant, two civilian PX workers who just started today."

Bowers lingered over one name: James Curtis . . . could it be the same one? He was aware that the Curtis he knew had taken some serious wounds. Could the world be that small? If it was the same Sergeant First Class James Curtis, then Ted had a score to settle. Revenge had become one of his delights during peacetime. He had conducted his retribution like a military campaign, carefully planning and executing tactics crafted to drive his personal enemy into miserable submission. Now he hoped it was Sgt. James Curtis; it would be a pleasure to torment his nemesis.

*****

"Private, over here on the double."

"Yes, Sergeant Bowers, on the double, Sergeant." A scrawny buck private dropped his broom and ran to Bowers, stopped and stood at attention. "Private Henderson reporting for duty, Sergeant."

Ted looked at the teenager. He couldn't be more than eighteen, maybe less if he had lied about his age to enlist. The kid looked at Bowers with wide eyes, full of trust and lacking any savvy.

Henderson was so eager to please he was like a puppy, but also as clumsy and naïve. He broke rules all the time without even knowing he was breaking them. The other soldiers always played practical jokes on the hapless boy. Now he had ten hours of cleaning duties for some offense Bowers didn't even remember.

"Private, how would you like to get cleared of your discipline duties?"

"Gee Sarge, that would be great . . . ah, I mean . . . Yes, Sergeant Bowers; whatever you say, Sergeant Bowers."

"Listen carefully, Private. I want you to walk over to the PX and look around. Ask some questions about what they're gonna have in the store. Then . . . listen closely to this . . . ask if any of them used to be in the army. Tell them . . . you're just curious about Korea, because you're going be stationed there next. Do not tell them I sent you. Do *not* mention my name. Stay long enough so it doesn't seem strange, but not too long. Do you understand? Repeat back my instructions."

Henderson barked out the orders precisely, his face eager with anticipation.

"Meet me at HQ when you're finished. Do not talk to anyone else. Are we clear?"

"Yes, Sergeant." The Private executed a snappy about-face and headed in the direction of the Post Exchange building.

Chapter 6
Rachel

Rob stared out over the small dune covered in beach grass, all that separated the cottage from Cape Cod Bay and a million-dollar view. Down at Cove Beach, Chickie Tyler's pickup sat next to Bobo Berrio's multi-colored, dilapidated heap with the wooden bumpers and mismatched tires.

"Boy, I hate to break the mood, but I promised Skip Parker I'd take over his traffic shift today. I better get changed."

While Rob was inside, Rachel wondered what it was that had caused her outburst. Shouldn't she be happy with the new changes in her life? She was finally back together with Rob, the only man she had ever truly loved. She was exhilarated with her college courses. Even though she was much older than almost all of her classmates, it was fun and challenging taking math and English classes again. She loved the discussions and exchange of intellectual ideas and enjoyed the comradery of the other students, although most were a little in awe of both her age and her obvious academic ability.

Maybe it was the realization that she would need to do at least three more years, counting summer classes, in order to get a degree. Then what? Did she need a college degree to get a job in Bound Brook? If she had wanted to teach, she would have, but she was getting a business degree. Meanwhile, what were she and Rob going to do? Could they handle three more years of a weekend romance? Should they get married? Okay, now she was jumping too far ahead of herself.

In the back of her mind was one problem she didn't share with Rob or anyone else; it was her English professor. Actually, he was an instructor, and was probably a little younger than she was. Charismatic and handsome, he was a popular teacher. At first, Rachel had been thrilled to be in his class. He had selected a theme of "Obsession and Vengeance" for the readings for the class. Shakespeare's *Hamlet*, Homer's *Iliad*, Melville's *Moby Dick* and Dumas' *The Count of Monte Cristo* were the core readings. Given the compressed nature of summer-school sessions, he had allowed students to use abridged versions of the longer works. The surprise had been when he had also assigned the comic book series, *Batman*.

Dr. Burke had used them all, to illustrate the universal theme and appeal of vengeance. His lectures on the topic of retribution had been like watching a theatrical production. The teacher's eyes would light up as he paced around like an actor on the stage. It was fun and motivating, and even the most reluctant students in his class left each session buzzing with enthusiastic comments.

He had pulled Rachel into his lectures so successfully that she had felt like he was aiming them at her personally. She still vividly remembered his introductory lecture:

"We will be reading plays, novels and mythology from different time periods and cultures. The classic themes of revenge and retribution have been part of recorded literature from the earliest times. I chose the works because we will be exploring the fine line between revenge and obsession, duty and fixation, retribution and madness.

"In Homer's Iliad, *how does Paris' obsession with Helen start an epic war? That story inspired Christopher Marlowe to write in* Doctor Faustus, *"Was this the face that launched a thousand ships?" Paris is not the only person driven by his own agenda. Was Achilles obsessed and if so by what? What drove Menelaus to mobilize a fleet of ships and send an army to avenge Helen's abduction?*

"Of course, that begs the question of whether Helen was abducted, seduced or willingly eloped. But, does it really matter to Menelaus what caused her to leave? Is he driven by love, jealousy, a need to show his power . . . or simply his wounded pride?

"Shakespeare has Hamlet speaking with a ghost who tells him, "Revenge his foul and most unnatural murder." Is Hamlet literally speaking with a ghost or has he already descended into lunacy?

"Speaking of insanity, what drives Ahab to pursue the White Whale to the exclusion of his real mission, which is supposed to be catching lots of whales and making money for the owners? Does his obsession lead to madness?

"Let's skip ahead to Batman and popular comic-book culture. As a boy, Bruce Wayne witnesses the murder of his parents and is scared for life. Backed by his immense inherited wealth, he embarks on a quest to root out evil and protect the innocent. Does it sound familiar? Batman could fit right in at King Arthur's Round Table. Or perhaps he could take the role of the Count of Monte Cristo, seeking retribution from those who have caused him great personal harm.

What is obsession? Is it a bad thing? What about the authors we are reading? Were they obsessed? I don't think you churn out multiple works of literature without a driving force, perhaps an obsession. Were the Wright Brothers obsessed? What about Henry Ford? Has any great achievement been possible without someone being obsessed?

For your first paper, I want you to take a position on whether obsession is necessary for success, or a dangerous state of mind. Choose one or more of our readings to illustrate your point. Oh, by the way, "Batman" cannot be your only source. You need to do a little more reading than just the comic book."

Rachel loved his class, and was pleased to learn that she would have him again in the fall for Business English. She had been pleased, but now she was worried. On the way out of the third meeting, a woman named Doris had walked up beside her.

"Well, well, well, is there something going on with you and the handsome professor?"

She was shocked. "What are you talking about?"

"It's obvious to everybody. The man only has eyes for you. It's like he is giving you a private tutorial, and the rest of us are just spectators."

Rachel couldn't even reply. What could she say?

"Hey, it could be a lot worse is what I say," Doris laughed. "You've got the looks and the smarts, why not use them."

It was true that Dr. Burke had taken an interest in Rachel, praising her essays and contributions to class discussions. He had referred to her as Miss Curtis and she had never bothered to correct him. She felt flattered by these compliments from a Ph.D. in English Literature, but she kept thinking about Doris's comments. Then in the last few classes, Dr. Burke's attention had gotten uncomfortable. He had lightly patted Rachel's back as he walked up and down the rows, reading passages from the classic novels.

On her way out of class one day, he had reached out and touched her arm. "I saw on your information that you come from Bound Brook on Cape Cod. What a coincidence, my family has a cottage in Truro. I grew up spending summers on the beach."

She just blushed. "Oh wow, that's funny."

He stared into her eyes. "Yes, the Cape is beautiful. Too bad I never ran into you."

"Yes, it's a small world. Ah . . . see you tomorrow, I've got to scoot."

For the remaining classes Rachel had felt extremely awkward as Dr. Burke's praises increased. He read sections of her essays aloud to the class, while Rachel had tried to slink under her desk. She remembered one in particular:

"I want to read you a portion of one essay that raises an interesting question. Miss Curtis writes, "The characters of Paris, Menelaus, Hector and Achilles are well developed and show their human characteristics. But what about Helen? The face that launched a thousand ships is an enigma. Is Helen a pawn in the game of war and power? Is she helpless or does she exert her own power, using her beauty to further her own goals. If the male rulers and warriors in The Iliad *are exalted as great warriors, what about the woman who is the central cause of the catastrophic war? In this essay I choose to explore the roles of the female characters in* The Iliad, *Helen and the goddesses—Hera, Athena and Aphrodite—who exert control over the male rulers of the ancient world."*

Miss Curtis goes on to develop a masterful essay from the female point of view. Truly one of the best papers I have had the privilege to read.

After the last class, he had asked her to stay behind to talk. "I'm very pleased to see that you are in my Business English class in the fall term. He paused and lowered his voice. "You know, you are the best student I've had since I started teaching here two years ago. I think you have great potential and I'd really love to mentor you."

"Why thank you. That's nice to hear."

He had reached out and patted her hand. "Why don't we go get a cup of coffee and talk about how I can help you?"

She did not even remember what she had said. Something about how she had to rush to catch the next train to Winchester. The whole exchange had left her uneasy. Was she reading too much into it and letting her imagination run wild?

But then, how did he know her permanent home address on the Cape? He would have had to make it a point to look it up.

She knew it was not all in her mind as she got back to her uncle and aunt's house in Winchester.

"Rachel, there was a phone call for you. I told him you weren't home yet," said Aunt Laura.

"Who was it?"

"He said he was your teacher. He said he hoped he'd run into you on the Cape during the break."

Rachel was stunned and her aunt gave her a curious look. The class roster didn't list her as Mrs. Curtis, and she had stopped wearing the little band Jimmy had given her when they had eloped. She didn't consider herself married anymore, even though the divorce wasn't final. However, she was committed to Rob and didn't want any other relationship, with her professor or anyone else. Next semester she would have to correct the impression that she was available. For now, she was not telling anyone about his attention. She just hoped she could avoid him on the Cape.

"Hey you, penny for your thoughts." Rob stood in front of the cottage dressed in his Bound Brook Police uniform.

"Oh nothing, just enjoying the view and wool gathering."

Rob leaned over her chair and gave her a kiss. "Stay and relax, you must be exhausted from final exams. After I get off duty, I have to meet with Ben about the cottage work, but do you want to catch a movie in Orleans tonight?"

"No thanks, I'd like to, but I think I owe my parents an evening home. Without them, I couldn't afford to pay for the classes. Besides, like you said, I think everything is catching up to me. I need an early night and lots of sleep."

"Okay, then how about going to the pond tomorrow? We can take Ben's boat out for a spin. I should work on the cottage, but I think it's going to be a hot day and it is the holiday week. Frankly, I can't think of a better reason to procrastinate."

"Sounds good."

She watched him drive off in his pickup. In some ways, he was an enigma. A gifted athlete, Ivy League graduate of Brown University, smart, level-headed and popular with everyone in town. However, he seemed to have no desire or ambition beyond being a part-time police officer, some occasional substitute teaching and helping with the basketball team. Rachel knew that life had left him with deep scars that didn't show.

Rob's mother had been unmarried when he was born, with his father nowhere in sight. His rich domineering grandfather had disowned his daughter when she had refused to have the baby in secret and give it up for adoption. At first, Roberta had been disgraced, but with the support of the Tyler clan and her own independence, she had won the admiration of the community.

Then she had drowned in a boating accident when Rob was thirteen. It had left Rob an orphaned bastard, rejected and ignored by his grandparents. Although he had become a basketball legend and been practically hero-worshipped in town, it must have left a mark. Was that why he was reluctant to put himself forward with more ambition? Was he afraid of rejection?

Rachel reminded herself of his other emotional wound. At the end of the war, Rob had been stationed in Marseille, France. He had been on Navy Shore Patrol duty when he saved Marie LaVache, a young French girl, from some drunken sailors. Her rich and powerful father had been grateful, taken Rob under his wing and encouraged their romance. When the war ended, he had given Rob a high-paying job and picked his brain about Navy shipping protocols and procedures. When Rob had discovered he was working for a criminal, and abetting him with smuggling, there had been a violent confrontation. He had been beaten, shipped back to the United States and given orders never to see Marie or her father again. Rachel believed the experience had bruised Rob's confidence and led him to hibernating in his safe little hometown.

At least his return had allowed them to be reunited. Rachel just needed to be more patient and let time take its course. She loved Rob, always had, and when you love someone you shouldn't try to change them.

As pleasant as it was sitting in the sun, she figured it was time to head home. However, she decided to make a quick stop in the town center to say hello to Mr. Williams at his pharmacy, where she had worked for years.

Chapter 7
Simon
Monday Morning

Once Simon Eldredge left the PX he drove around, killing time. He lived in a rooming house in the neighboring town of Bound Brook, a pretty location near the town pier. So it was at the pier where he parked and admired the scenery of Bound Brook Harbor. The sun shone off the calm bay and the boats created a scene like a beautiful painting. Fishermen busied themselves with their tasks, another reminder that he didn't fit in.

Simon knew he was incompetent, he had heard it his whole life. The extended Eldredge clan of Yarmouth were sturdy, steady, reliable and competent—except Simon. He couldn't help it. When he should be focused on simple mundane tasks, his mind wandered. He considered the scenery, words played around in his mind, ideas flew in and out, and soon the task was forgotten.

He fidgeted with the Bulova watch on his wrist. It was the object of his earlier search. He had gotten a letter that said Bulova was sending a complimentary watch to the store manager, and hoped that he would wear it and recommend it to his customers. Even though he trusted George Gilmore, habit had forced him to grab it before anyone else took it. Simon was the youngest of seven and the runt of the litter. All his life, five older brothers and one sister had pushed him around, and always grabbed the best of everything.

He was relieved to be out of the store. When he was at the PX, his anxiety level drove his pulse to a pounding level and he couldn't think or talk straight. He knew he was ill suited to manage a store. It had always been that way growing up in his family. His older brothers were rugged and athletic, and had a practical sense of how to do tasks they were given by their father. Chandler Eldredge ran a grain, feed and hardware store in Yarmouth, and his older sons were all in some type of building trade. Even Simon's sister, just a year older, was practical and pragmatic.

His father was a hard man. The epitome of a crusty Cape Codder, Chandler Eldredge did not tolerate what he considered "sinful behavior." Idleness, swearing or lying would get you a hard smack across your rear-end. One day, two kids tried to sneak out of the store with some toy yoyos, kept near the cash register. When Chandler caught them, he dragged them to their parents' house.

"If you don't paddle them, I will," he bellowed. "Nobody steals from an Eldredge!"

Simon had been a disappointment to his father and a nuisance to his siblings. He had messed up everything they asked him to do. He miscounted the grain store inventory, he hammered his thumb and bent nails, he dropped fragile boxes, spilled bags of feed, mixed up the pricing labels . . . and generally proved his uselessness in all endeavors.

It wasn't that he didn't try, he really tried hard, maybe too hard. Halfway through counting the inventory, he would get distracted and lose track. His father would yell, "what's taking you so long?" as Simon panicked. Then he couldn't think straight and would just make a wild guess.

It had been the same way in school. Teachers rolled their eyes at his lack of attention. Only in art or music had Simon felt relaxed and focused. However, the Eldredge family were not artists or musicians, and neither were most families in Yarmouth. They were practical people who needed to make a living.

The only thing he could do that was slightly athletic was hitting baseballs to his brothers. All of them played baseball and were very good. His brother Ralph was three years older and insisted that Simon help him practice by hitting fungos to him. At first, Simon was terrible, but eventually he got the knack and spent hours hitting grounders and fly balls to his brother. Too bad he couldn't hit the ball when a pitcher threw it to him.

The PX was now Simon's last chance to prove himself. His sister had an important job with the company that managed the Post Exchanges for the army, and she had pulled a few strings to get him the position. She had even sold him her old 1941 Studebaker two-door coupe for forty bucks. Of course, he owed her the money until he got his first paycheck. She even joked, "This Studebaker model is called the Champion, maybe it'll bring you luck."

Honestly, not many wanted the PX job. It was only for the summer, and had little chance for advancement, but Simon was desperate. Now he realized how foolish he had been, just one more in a long list of failures.

Simon had never been in charge of anything. He had no idea how to be a manager. Part of him knew he was being a jerk, trying to assert his authority by issuing meaningless orders. His one hope was George Gilmore. George was not only capable, but also kind and patient. If Simon could get through the summer without messing up, maybe he could prove something to his family.

Meanwhile, he tried to avoid the store as much as possible. He dreaded the day the first flood of National Guardsmen would invade the PX. He hated to admit it, but his best approach was to stay away. He wouldn't be pulling his weight, but at least there was less he could screw up.

It was time to head back to Camp Wellfleet, but Simon took the scenic route along Bound Brook Creek, into the town center. Bound Brook was a pretty hamlet in an old-fashioned, hardworking, fishing-village way. It was like his hometown of Yarmouth, but also different. The Mid-Cape had Cape Cod Bay and Nantucket Sound, but the Outer Cape had the powerful Atlantic Ocean.

Simon had been awed when he had first arrived at Camp Wellfleet. The flat wind-swept sand looked like a desert that ended with steep dune cliffs overlooking the pounding surf of what the natives called "The Backshore." Nearby were the remains of the Marconi Wireless site, the location of the first transatlantic wireless signal sent to England. The desolate area was bordered on the north by a marsh: a boggy thicket of dense shrubs and tall hardwood cedar trees—a foreboding sight that tickled Simon's imagination while raising the hair on the back of his neck. If a soldier wanted to go AWOL, the swamp was not a good route.

A policeman, directing traffic, waved Simon ahead, but a dark sedan pulled out of the Town Hall parking lot in front of his car. Too late, Simon slammed on the brakes and blew his horn. A white-haired woman looked at him with surprise as her car stopped halfway out in the street. The crunch and metal screech were like fingernails on the blackboard to Simon's ears. The police officer blew his whistle and pedestrians stopped and stared. It was like his worst nightmare; here he was again, a total screw-up.

*****

Sergeant Bowers sat at the counter in Agnes' Restaurant in Bound Brook Center, scanning the blackboard specials. Private Henderson had completed his mission in a reasonably satisfactory manner. Despite his jumbled report, it was enough for Ted to confirm that James Curtis was a Sergeant, recently medically discharged from Korea. Bowers knew from the sign-in sheet at the gate that Curtis lived in Bound Brook. Now he was on a reconnaissance mission, dressed in civvies and gathering intelligence at the type of place that specialized in local gossip.

Agnes' was a local hangout Ted had visited a few weeks before for a Sunday breakfast. The half-dozen tables were filled with the lunch crowd, but the action was at the counter where five local men drank coffee and ate sandwiches while trading good-natured insults. Their Cape Cod accents were so thick that Ted missed some of the conversation.

"Excuse me, I'm new here, any recommendations?"

The man next to him turned and gave him a skeptical look. "It's all good. Burgers are thick, but I like the roast beef sandwiches. What service you in?"

Ted laughed. "I guess dressing in civvies doesn't hide much. What was it, the hair cut?"

"Well, that, but the shiny shoes and neat pressed pants don't fit in much 'round here. Besides we know everybody in this town and half the Cape."

The man laughed and exposed one missing canine tooth. He and his companions were dressed in work clothes, due for a wash. A ruddy weather-beaten face made him seem much older, but on a closer look, Ted realized they were around the same age.

"I'm in the army, but just passing through. I think I remember a buddy from Korea who lives in this town. You know James Curtis?"

The man laughed. "Hey guys, he wants to know if we know Jimmy Curtis."

The other men joined in with chuckles. "Mister, everybody knows Jimmy. Big war hero now. They gave him a bunch of medals. Course, he walks with a gimp and salutes with three fingers now. Don't think he's gonna be playing much basketball no more."

The second man down joined in. "He got a job over at Camp Wellfleet at the PX. I suppose you could look him up there if you wanted."

"I probably don't have time, but maybe."

"What's your name? When I see him, I'll tell him you asked."

"Simmons," Ted replied quickly, with the first name that came to mind. "Corporal Ted Simmons, probably doesn't remember me. I was just another buck private, but you tend to remember the sergeants."

"Well Corporal Simmons, I'm Bunky Morris and this here is Honk Snow. Them others are Tricky Tyler, Davey Sousa, and the big lug at the end is Moose Parker. Half of us is the highway department and the others fish."

"So, is Curtis married or have a family?"

Bunky looked uncomfortable. "Just his mother. Well technically he's still married to Rachel Gilmore, but they's gettin' a divorce. I expect Rachel will be marrying Rob Caldwell now, once she's free."

A screech of brakes, and the blast of a car horn, followed by crash and crunch sounds, interrupted the conversation.

Everyone at the counter, including Ted, moved to the door and onto the sidewalk.

"Looks like your brother is gonna have his hands full, Moose."

"Ain't that the Widow Sousa's car?" the man named Honk pointed.

"Sure is," replied Bunky. "She's about the worst driver in town. She drives real slow, but she don't stop for signs. She had that accident with Bobby Snow this winter. Amazing she don't have more."

"Not familiar with the other car, but I expect my brother will sort it all out," said Moose.

Chapter 8
Police Work
Ted

Rob parked in the lot down by the Catholic Church. Out on Main Street he saw a crowd gathered in the middle of the road in front of the Town Hall. It looked like a two-car accident, with Special Officer Skip Parker listening to the drivers. One driver was the Widow Sousa, not a surprise.

"But Mrs. Sousa, I held my hand up for you to stop," said Skip.

"Why Skippy, I thought you were just waving at me."

"I slammed on my brakes as fast as I could," said a pale, thin young man.

"Well, once I saw him comin', I stopped," said the Widow.

Skip shook his head. "Yes, ma'am, but that was in the middle of the street."

It was all Rob could do to keep from laughing. The Widow Sousa was an accident waiting to happen, a sweet old lady, but a public menace. Sometimes she drove so far over to the side of the road that she clipped the sidewalks and almost hit the telephone poles.

"Hi, Skip. How do you want to handle this? Want me to redirect traffic while you get their information? I can have cars turn around in the parking lot and go back the other way."

"I think someone can back Mrs. Sousa's car into the lot. That will give us one lane. I don't think this gentleman's car is going anywhere."

Skip yelled over to the men outside Agnes', "Hey, Davey Sousa, you want to back your aunt's car off the road?

Moose, can you go in and ask Agnes to call Proctor's Garage for the tow truck?"

****

Ted Bowers stood on the sidewalk next to Bunky Morris. "So who's who?"

"The first cop is Skip Parker, Moose's brother. The lady is the Widow Sousa, she is Davey's aunt, and the other officer is Rob Caldwell, the guy I mentioned to you. The other driver is someone I don't know."

Ted noticed an attractive redhead walking toward the accident. "Who's the chick?"

Bunky gave him a frown, "Oh that's Rachel. She's getting divorced from that guy you was asking about, Jimmy Curtis. The other cop, Rob, is the one she's probably gonna marry next."

Ted smiled; this was better than he could have hoped. He used the confusion of the accident as a chance to slip away. He walked down a side lane to his army Jeep and drove the back way out of the center. Out on Route 6 he thought about the new information. The best way to hurt people was through their friends and family. Meanwhile, he planned to conduct some harassment raids.

Back on the base, Ted returned the Jeep to the HQ lot. He walked over to the most recent building construction, keeping his eyes on the ground. Then he saw one; he stooped and picked up a long galvanized nail. He spotted another one and added it to his pocket. He worked his way over to the back of the PX and saw three cars parked against the building. The license plate on an older sedan matched the number from Curtis' sign-in sheet at the guard gate.

Ted checked to make sure nobody was around, then slipped down the right side of the sedan and stooped next to the passenger front tire. He took a nail, jammed the point into the bottom rear of the tire tread and wedged the head into the pavement. Then he repeated the process on the rear tire. When Curtis backed out of the parking space, the nails would puncture the tires and work their way into the inner tubes. Most cars had a spare tire, but Bowers doubted Curtis had two. With so much construction work, it would look like a simple accident.

Tonight he planned to check out the PX again. When the contractors had completed the building they had given him the keys, and he had kept one for himself before passing along the rest to the skinny, nervous manager. If anyone had asked, it was for "base security reasons."

Chapter 9
Jim - Out of Commission
Monday Afternoon

George screwed the top back onto his thermos bottle and brushed the sandwich crumbs off his hands. Jimmy and Benny had made great progress and the PX was starting to look like a real store.

"Excuse me, sir, are you George Gilmore?" A young enlisted man stood in the doorway.

"I'm George. What can I do for you?"

"Sir, I have a message for you from Mr. Eldredge."

George took a slip of message paper from the soldier.

Car accident won't be in today. I'm at the doctor. Not sure about tomorrow. – Simon

Jimmy glanced at the paper. "What's that?"

"Sounds like Simon had a fender-bender and won't be coming back today, maybe not tomorrow either."

"I hope he's alright."

George nodded. "Me too. Hate to say it, but we'll probably get more work done without him."

The three men worked hard through the afternoon and by 4:45 they had all the shelves assembled and in place. Tomorrow they could start on stocking the products.

"Okay, guys, time to clean up and call it a day." Jimmy and Ben tidied up their areas and put away their tools. "You guys can head along. I'll lock up." Ben and Jimmy went out the back door to the paved parking lot.

"Jimmy, I almost forgot, can I get a ride with you tomorrow? My mom needs the car."

"Sure, I'll pick you up about 8:40."

"Thanks," said Ben, getting in his family's sedan. Jim waved as he backed out of the space and turned onto the main road of the Camp.

Nice kid, he thought. Being around Ben reminded him of his own carefree high school days: Hanging out with Rob, Hoopy and Rachel; and playing basketball with Rob, Hoopy, Jerry Tyler, Johnny Sousa and Moose Parker, coached by George Gilmore. Rob had been the star, a tall, gifted player, but Hoopy and Jimmy had been good enough to make the Cape League All-Star second team. Now there was nothing but faded memories.

Jim put in the clutch, started the car and shifted into reverse. There was a crunching pop sound; probably drove over a shell dropped by one of the many seagulls. The guard waved as he slowed at the gate. He turned right on to Route 6 and accelerated. Then . . . *Bang!* . . . Followed by the distinctive flap, flap, flap sound of a flat tire. He pulled over to the weedy shoulder of the road. He got out with a sigh and glanced at the driver's side tires that looked fully inflated. On the passenger side, it was a different story; the rear was flat as a pancake. The end of a nail protruded from the tread.

He popped open the trunk and checked for his mother's spare. *Geez, I hope that isn't flat too! Who knows how long it's been sitting there?* He pulled out the tire and bounced it on the ground. Good, it should do the trick. Next, he extracted the jack and tire iron. He knelt beside the tire, his stiff left knee protesting the move. As he wedged the hubcap off, he heard a hissing sound coming from the front.

"Damn!" He glanced forward. The front tire was already half deflated.

Beep, Beep came the sound as George Gilmore's Chevy eased behind the Chrysler. "Need a hand?"

"More like I need a ride. Never had two flats at the same time before. I think the carpenters better be more careful with their nails."

"Might as well just leave it. I'll give you a lift to Hooper's Garage."

Jimmy got in the passenger seat and George eased back out onto the highway. Being alone with his father-in-law, he felt awkward. "Coach, we haven't had a chance to talk about things, man-to-man. I just wanted you to know that I still think the world of Rachel. I've been a rotten husband, and don't deserve her. I know now, I never should have taken her from Rob. It wasn't right. I just hope, somehow, that you and Mrs. Gilmore can forgive me."

"Jim, there's nothing to forgive. Rachel made her own decisions, right or wrong. Life isn't perfect, and we all have to make the best of what happens. Maggie and I will always be fond of you, no matter what."

The Chevy passed through Wellfleet and into Bound Brook as they sat in silence. Near the entrance to Bound Brook Center, a red flying horse, Pegasus, marked Hooper's Flying A service station. George pulled in and parked beside the office.

Harold Hooper stood at a row of three red pumps, putting gas into Rob Caldwell's pickup truck. He waved. "My little brother and Rob are in the office."

"Thanks," said George.

Jimmy hesitated, then spoke softly. "Ain't talked to Rob in a long time."

George got out of the car. "Well, no time like the present."

"I guess."

A bell jingled as the two opened the door to find Horace "Hoopy" Hooper and Rob, still in his police uniform, in the cramped office, drinking Coca Colas from the garage's machine.

Hoopy nodded at the pair. "Well, well, what's going on with you two?"

"Jimmy managed to get two flat tires at the same time out by Camp Wellfleet."

"Hmmm, that might set some sort of record. Let me get the tow truck, and I'll bring it back here and get it fixed."

"You'll need to finish changing the rear tire. There's a good spare right there. I started to change it, but when I saw the front was going flat, I got kinda deflated too."

"Service with a smile. I should be back in about 30 minutes, and can probably get it fixed tonight. I'll just call the wife and tell her to hold supper. Won't be the first time. Meanwhile have a Coke on me." Hoopy flipped Jim the machine key.

George approached Rob. "So, anything exciting in Bound Brook today, Officer Caldwell?"

"Actually, George, we had an accident in the center. Think you know one of the people, Simon Eldredge? He said he was the manager of the Post Exchange at Camp Wellfleet. Accident wasn't really his fault. Widow Sousa did it again. Pulled out of the Town Hall parking lot, ignored Skip Parker's signal to stop, and then when she did stop it was in the middle of the road. She said she thought Skip was waving at her to say hello," he chuckled.

"I got a message from Simon that he got hurt. How bad did it seem to you?"

"Nothing visible, but I suspect he will ache all over, probably got some whiplash."

"Well, that'll be the talk of the town for a few days," laughed Jimmy.

"George," Rob offered, "I can give Jimmy a lift if he needs one. You can head home,"

George gave Jim a look. "That sounds like a good idea. I think you two might have some things to talk about."

After George and Hoopy left, Rob just looked at Jimmy for a moment and then laughed. "Seems like the Gilmore clan have the same idea that we need to talk. Rachel's been bugging me too."

"Well, they're right. . . . Let me start. I am so sorry for what I did to you. I knew you and Rachel loved each other, but I was selfish. When she turned to me, I couldn't resist. You were my best friend, but now I know that I was just jealous. I loved her too, and you . . . well, you are just so damn perfect; the best basketball player I ever saw. Add to that, you're smart, tall and handsome . . . Man, you could have any girl you want. Me, I'm just a backstabbing cheat!"

"Whoa, you're too hard on yourself. I'm the one that screwed up with Elaine Samuels. Nobody made me do that."

"You were drunk, and Elaine was hard to resist. She always had a thing for you."

"I guess there's nothing either of us can do about it. The past is the past, and we both need to get beyond it. Anyway, Rachel and I are together now. Time to move on. I appreciate your apology, but there's really no need. And what you've done in your army career . . . Wow, you sell yourself too short!"

Jim shrugged. "The army is the only thing I've done right, and now that's over."

The two former friends fell silent.

Harold opened the door. "Hey you two, am I interrupting something? My brother said you have some tire trouble."

"Yep, my mother's car. That reminds me, I want to talk to you about getting my own wheels. You have anything that's a few years old for a good price?"

"There's a '47 Packard out back that I got in a trade. You can try it out for a few days, see if you like it."

"Okay, let me take a look."

"I'd like to see it too," said Rob.

The three men went out back where there were three older cars, two of them obviously needing repairs. A dark-blue one gleamed from a fresh wash and wax.

Jimmy whistled. "This is a Packard Clipper, Harold; it must cost a pretty penny? I can't afford something that nice."

Harold smiled. "Well, I got it in exchange for something cheaper and to pay off an outstanding bill. Really didn't cost me anything out of pocket. It's in great shape, but it is five years old. Don't worry about the price, we'll work it out. Least I can do for a war hero."

"No, no, I'm not cashing in on the war. I did what lots of other guys have done. Look at your brother; he had it tough in the Italian Campaign in WWII. He had to sit on that beach at Anzio and get shelled by German cannons for weeks. All because of some dumb general's lack of initiative."

"I know and when I think about guys like you two, I feel guilty that a bad lung x-ray kept me at home. You guys deserve a little break here and there. Hoopy doesn't like to talk about it, but I know he still has bad dreams about the war. What about you?"

"Yeah, but I don't like to talk about it either. It was pretty bad. Talk about guilt, I feel guilty that I'm not still over there. I still feel responsible for my men, you know, as if I should be there watching out for them. I know it makes no sense, but there is no tighter bond than with men in battle. The closest was when we played basketball, but that's a game; in war, it's life or death." Without thinking, Jim flexed the remaining fingers of his left hand.

"Look, take the car for now, after all it's just sitting here. That way Hoopy can fix the tires tomorrow; he'll get home in time for dinner and you have wheels. We can talk about a price later."

*****

"Hi, Mom," said Rachel. "Can I talk to you about something."

"Sure, Rachel," Maggie Gilmore replied. "What is it?"

"I'm really confused right now. I'm not sure what I want to do."

Maggie stopped drying dishes and turned to her daughter. "Confused about what?"

"Well . . . college, Rob, Jimmy, Bound Brook . . . just everything."

Maggie put down the dishcloth. "Let's sit down and you can tell me about it." She dropped into a chair. "Let's start with college. You did great this semester, so what's the problem?"

"I always wanted to go to college, and part of me has felt incomplete that I ran off with Jimmy and never went to Bridgewater State to be a teacher. So, going to BU for this summer session is like a dream come true, or at least I thought it was."

"Rachel, I thought you really enjoyed your classes."

"Yes, I did, they were great. I don't know, now that they're over, I've been wondering. What am I going to do with a college degree? I mean, part of the fun this semester was proving to myself that I could do college work. Well, I knew I could, but maybe I had to prove it. Now I know I can, in fact I got A grades. Now I wonder if it is worth spending three or more years, traipsing back and forth to Boston, just to say I have a Bachelor's Degree."

"Is this about Rob?"

"No . . . Well, maybe yes, I mean partly. I was naïve. I thought, finally Jimmy and I are getting divorced and we don't have to pretend we have a real marriage anymore. Rob and I could get back together, and it would be just like to was supposed to be twelve years ago. Rob would wait for me while I got my college degree and we would be together, happily ever after. The perfect fairytale. Now I wonder. I love Rob, but I think our relationship is going to need work."

"So, are you afraid he won't wait?"

"No, I know he'll wait. Rob is like a faithful dog. That's not an insult; I mean I think he's been waiting for me all this time. Just marking time, waiting patiently in case someday I would be free. Now, I don't know if it's fair to make him wait more while we have a part-time romance, just so I can check college off my to-do list."

Maggie nodded. "Yes, I see what you mean. I think you're right about Rob too."

The words came gushing out of Rachel: "You know, neither of us has had a real mature relationship. I ran off with Jimmy because I was hurt and he was a good friend. We were eighteen and played at being married for a couple of years. It was fun; mostly we partied with our friends. Then World War Two broke out, Jimmy enlisted and was gone for almost four years.

"When he came back, he was . . . different. The war changed him. He started drinking too much, and we didn't really have a marriage. I think we were both thinking about separating when Korea happened. Then he was off to war again. What hurt the most was, he was happy to be leaving. I had been thinking about getting a divorce, but then he left.

"I didn't want to send a Dear John letter to a soldier in combat. It wouldn't be fair. I look back now and realize that in twelve years of marriage, we were only together half that time. For six out of the twelve, I've been on my own. And then he sent me that letter from Korea, saying he thought we should get divorced. Boy, it was a relief!"

Her mother frowned. "I think you and Jimmy were a mistake, but it is true you never had much of a chance to try to make it work. Certainly his drinking made it harder."

"And then I ask myself: why college? Rob and I both want to stay on Cape Cod. You know, when some of the other students found out I live in Bound Brook, they asked why I would ever want to leave. I'm smart. I'm capable. I know I could get a good job on the Cape without a degree, so why would I waste three more years?"

Maggie smiled and patted her hand. "I know you and Rob love each other, but you bring up a good point. It takes more than love to have a good marriage. You both have to work at it. I can see that if you are going to college full-time, then you and Rob don't have much time to work on a relationship."

"Exactly, and there's something else I've been thinking about. You know it didn't take long to figure out that Jimmy was not the best husband and we would never have a good marriage. Well, I never thought about having children with him. I took precautions most of the time, but sometimes we didn't, and . . . well, I've never gotten pregnant. I mean that was good, I guess, but now I wonder if I can."

"Would you like to have children with Rob?"

"Yes, I would, but I've never talked with him about it. I think he'd like children. It's just I'm not getting any younger, and if I spend three years going to college maybe I'll never have kids. I just don't know if it's worth it. It was different when I was eighteen."

"Well, you have the rest of the summer to think about it. If you don't want to go back to BU in September, that's fine. It's your choice."

"Thanks, Mom." She paused before continuing with the issue she'd been keeping inside. "There is one other thing. It's not life changing or a big part of what I decide, but something happened with one of my college teachers, and I don't know what to do about it."

Then she told her mother about Dr. Peter Burke's particular interest in her. Maggie listened, her face reflecting a growing concern.

Chapter 10
Peter – Obsession
Tuesday Morning

George Gilmore arrived at the PX at 7:00, even earlier than usual. With Simon still recovering from his accident, he wanted to make sure they stayed ahead of the scheduled opening day, now less than a week away. Simon had called him last night and said he was sore all over, with a stiff neck and back. George had reassured him that things would be fine, but he could tell that Simon was nervous and worried. Of course, nervous and worried was Simon's natural state.

Before he unlocked the building, he took a moment to admire his surroundings. The contractors hadn't arrived yet, and the soldiers were eating breakfast in the large tent that served as the temporary chow hall. The sun was low in the east over the Atlantic Ocean with the hush and stillness of dawn still in the air.

Camp Wellfleet spread out over a barren flat expanse of sand. The arid soil and exposure to the northeast storms and salt spray had left the vast area undeveloped for years. An eerie white cedar forest and swamp marked the northern border. The combination of isolation and spooky marsh had led the early pilgrim settlers to label the area "The Devil's Pasture" and "Lucifer's Land."

Around 1900 when Guglielmo Marconi had needed a location to build the transmission towers for the first transatlantic radio message sent to England, Wellfleet had been ideal. Remnants of the towers remained today, but the relentless ocean had eroded the steep dunes and carved into the historic location. Useless for farming and too exposed for housing, the area had remained desolate. George remembered a local story about the message from President Teddy Roosevelt and the reply from the King of England.

He chuckled to himself as he recalled the details. When Marconi had gotten the reply from King Edward, he had run out to Charlie Paine. Charlie was waiting with his horse, Diamond, to relay the response to the telegraph office in Orleans, where it would be forwarded to President Roosevelt.

"Drive like the wind, and if you kill your horse I'll buy you a new one," yelled the ecstatic Marconi.

Well, Charlie was a practical Cape Codder. He whipped Diamond to full speed, but as soon as he was out of sight, he slowed to a more modest pace.

When asked about this later, Charlie had said, "I was excited too, but I wasn't going to kill my horse—not even for Marconi, the King of England or the President of the United States."

There were those who doubted the veracity of Charlie's tale. In fact, some said the telegraph office in Orleans had been closed that day. However, Charlie stuck with his story and in George's opinion sometimes a good tall tale was better than the facts. It certainly made the history more interesting.

When the army had needed a base for anti-aircraft training in World War II, it was the perfect location. Opening in 1943, the base had buzzed with activity, as a thousand soldiers and scores of buildings dotted the landscape. A line of towers had sprung from the edge of the dunes, with lines of anti-aircraft cannons pointing their barrels over the Atlantic. Airplanes had towed target sleeves over the water and artillery shells fell into the ocean. After the war, the buildings had been demolished and the base abandoned. Now, only a few years later, it was coming back to life.

George unlocked the door and surveyed the store. Jimmy and Benny had assembled most of the shelving and counters, and today he hoped they could start stocking the products into their departments. He walked along the stacks of cartons and stopped at the huge stack of cigarettes. Every brand he could think of was represented: Pall Mall, Lucky Strike, Camel, Marlboro, Chesterfield, Kent, Viceroy, all the major names.

He stopped. Something seemed different compared to yesterday. There were seven evenly stacked sets of cartons. He counted from the bottom: five cartons high. Was he confused, or had the piles been six cartons high when he had left? He'd check with the others when they arrived. Meanwhile he moved on to the watches and jewelry.

*****

"I'll race you. Give you a three second lead. Ready?"

Rachel nodded to Rob, dove into the brisk water of Bound Brook Pond and broke into a strong crawl stroke.

"One one-thousand, two one-thousand, three, here I come."

She heard the splash and pushed her stroke even harder. Ben Brown's small motorboat was moored only twenty yards from shore, so it wasn't much of a race. She reached out for the gunwale a second before Rob. "Beat you!"

"Next time you only get two seconds."

"I'll still beat you," laughed Rachel.

"So, do you want to fish or just ride around the pond?"

"Well, there's Horse Pond the other side of the sluiceway. I seem to remember a private little beach there." She gave him a wink.

"Excuse me, I feel like I'm about to be seduced."

"Only if you want to be. Of course we could just go swimming if you'd rather."

"No, no, I'm willing to oblige your wishes. So, I guess I could do that."

"Well, I appreciate you making the sacrifice."

Rob gave her a big smirk. He yanked the cord on Ben's tiny fishing motor and the engine kicked on. He switched the engine to forward and they puttered out into the pond.

Away from the shore there was a morning chill, but Rob could sense the beginnings of summer heat starting to build. The sun had burned the early morning mist off the pond, but a haze lingered along some spots on the shore where the dense vegetation cast a shadow over the water.

It was only nine in the morning on a weekday and the pond was deserted. Too early for the swimmers, but late enough that any early-morning anglers had already left. Over his shoulder, he eyed the swimming beach and the wooden raft. To its left was the boat ramp for transient launching. In another week, the beach would be teeming with activity when the Town Recreation Program started the summer swimming lessons for youngsters.

He headed the boat toward the opposite shore, where he could just make out a break in the trees that marked their target. The sluiceway was a narrow channel that almost connected Bound Brook Pond with the smaller and weedier Horse Pond. They could beach the boat and walk the fifty feet or, with a little muscle, pull the boat through the six inches of water.

"My father told me you saw Jim yesterday. Did you get a chance to talk?"

"Sure, we talked."

"Okay, how about some details?"

"He said he was sorry for what he did and how he's treated you. I told him it was my fault for getting involved with Elaine. That was about it."

"Men! That was it? You call that a talk? What else did he say?"

"Not much. Hoopy was off towing his mother's car. I guess your Dad must have told you about his flat tires. Anyway, Harold came in and we started talking about the war. Jimmy talked a little about Korea, but not much. Said he felt guilty that he wasn't still there watching out for his men. Then he said he needed to buy a used car, and Harold showed him a nice Packard Clipper, a real beauty. He suspected Harold was going to sell it to him too cheap and tried to refuse, but Harold talked him into trying it out. Then he drove home. That's it."

Rachel shook her head. "So you men talked about war and cars. I bet you spent less than a minute talking about unimportant things, like what happened with me and how you two best friends haven't talked to each other in twelve years. You know, the little stuff, not as important as automobiles. Just twelve years of hurt feelings and missed opportunities, but nothing really significant."

Rob shrugged. "Well, it was a start." Rachel just turned and stared over the bow of the boat.

He knew he'd messed up. He really didn't know anything about relationships. He had been living a quiet life since his return from France, with a few brief and uncomplicated dating affairs in the past years, but nothing lasting. His only two love affairs, with Rachel and the French girl, Marie, had both ended badly, and had left him wary. Now he felt like a bumbling teenager. Rachel obviously had expectations for how he should behave; he just wished he knew what they were.

She turned and gave him a smile. "I'm sorry. I can't expect you and Jimmy to act like I would. You're right, it was a start. I'm glad the two of you are speaking again. It's just . . .

I'll never understand men. You talk about cars, sports, and war, but when it comes to relationships? Nothing."

"You'll never understand men? Wow, I'll tell you I think women are even more of a mystery. Maybe that's what sparks the chemistry."

Rachel laughed. "Yes, I think you'd be a lot less appealing if you acted like Cindy Morris or one of my other girlfriends."

Rob cut the motor and let the boat drift into the shallow opening of the sluiceway. Rachel jumped out, grabbed the bowline and pulled them ashore. He admired her trim, athletic figure. Her one-piece white Catalina swimsuit only accented her curves and tanned legs. He stepped into the clear water and helped her pull the small craft through the opening until it emerged onto Horse Pond.

The isolated pond had more lily pads and weeds than Bound Brook Pond. However, two small sandy beach areas were weed free. Trees and bushes grew to the edge of the shore around the rest of the circular pool. Only a few locals ever used the pond, and tourists didn't even know it existed.

Rachel ran in up to her knees and dove. Several second later, she surfaced and stood shoulder deep in the still water. Rob watched while she slipped the straps of her suit over her shoulders and then dipped under the surface. When she popped up, she had something in her hands.

"I'll trade you my suit for yours."

Rob didn't wait. He slipped off his trunks, waded in and tossed them in her direction.

"Here, catch!"

Then he dove and, with powerful breaststrokes, swam underwater until his eyes took in the tan legs and white body. He put his arms around her waist, surfaced and squirted water in her face. She laughed and pushed him away.

"What are you, thirteen years old? I was expecting a little more romance."

He reached out and pulled her close. She returned the hug and snuggled against his bare chest. With the tips of his fingers, he cupped her chin and tilted her head up to his waiting mouth.

Still deep in their kiss, Rob bent his knees into a crouch as she floated onto his lap. She reached down and guided him. Weightless, she rocked her body as their passion rose.

*****

Peter Burke Ph.D. had found her house the day before. In a small town, it wasn't hard to ask a few questions and get directions. Around six o'clock he drove to the Gilmore home. He parked in an empty driveway across the street, about fifty yards away. Pine trees partially blocked his 1948 Willys Jeepster from view. With the cover off and a stack of 2x4s and boards in the back, it looked like any typical Cape Cod handyman's vehicle.

In her driveway was an ancient two-door coupe, so someone must be home. He didn't wait very long before a sedan pulled into her driveway. A fit looking older man got out of the car and went inside, obviously her father. The anticipation got him excited, but nobody came out of the house. After thirty minutes, he drove away. He considered calling her parents' house, but he liked following her even better. Tomorrow he would wait for her. The thrill was more in the chase.

He got to her house around eight o'clock in the morning, and the sedan was already gone. He finally got his reward when Rachel came out of the door about thirty minutes later. She wore jean shorts over a white bathing suit and carried a small bag and towel. She backed onto the street and he ducked as she drove past. He gave her a head start and then pulled out and followed. The roads were almost empty, so it was easy to keep her in sight. Besides, he had a hunch that he knew where she was going.

Rachel drove through the northern edge of the town center and headed out to the highway. She took a left toward Truro and Provincetown, but in a mile turned right onto Bound Brook Pond Road. He knew the pond from his childhood years. It was one of the prettiest and best swimming spots in the area. Now he dropped back further and took a left at a well-used dirt road.

By the time he edged into the opening of the large, packed-earth parking lot, Rachel was out of the car and in the arms of a very tall young man. The two kissed and then holding hands went down the embankment. He backed up and turned onto a narrow dirt road to the left. The rutted lane followed the north shoreline and led to a small parking lot at what the locals called "the sluiceway." He drove slowly and through gaps in the shrubbery, he caught sight of two figures in a small boat. The sound of a small outboard motor filtered through the leaves. The boat headed slowly toward an opening at the northern shore of the pond.

He drove cautiously down the rutted one-lane pathway until it widened, just before it came to an abrupt end. The wide area served as a makeshift parking lot. With some creativity, six to eight cars could squeeze between the scrub pine and stunted oaks. He got out of the Jeep and closed the door quietly. A path led through a copse of trees and a hint of blue water was barely visible.

He stopped before the path opened onto a sandy beach and warily parted the thick shrubs. Crouching, he crept forward until he could see the pond from his hidden vantage point.

The two were in the water, locked in a deep embrace. Rachel gripped the man's shoulders and rocked her body. The man pulled her into a deep kiss and she tightened her hold. The rocking grew more intense. Then Rachel pulled away from his kiss, threw her head back with a deep moan and collapsed in the man's arms.

His own breathing quickened and his pulse soared. He closed his eyes and pictured himself in the pond with her. Then his arousal peaked and he stifled a deep sigh. Gradually his breathing slowed as he became aware of his surroundings. The couple were laughing and splashing each other, their swimsuits still floating in the water.

He eased out of the thick vegetation and made his way back to his car. Before he started the engine, he visualized the scene once again. The image burned in his memory and excitement mixed with jealousy. He had longed for her from the first minute. He knew he was fixated, but it was a feeling he craved. He knew he had to have her.

The car turned and started down the shady lane.

Chapter 11
Ted - Past Crimes
Wednesday, Five Hundred Hours

Bowers snapped awake. It was still dark, but he knew a hint of dawn would be peeking over the edge of the Atlantic Ocean. Ted's internal alarm clock always woke him up just after five hundred hours, almost an hour ahead of the recorded bugle reveille that sounded over the camp. He treasured the quiet time before the hubbub of soldiers waking up, washing up and eating in the chow hall. It gave him a chance to stay one step ahead of the officers and his men.

However, this morning he felt groggy from a rough night of bad dreams. Discovering that Sergeant Curtis was on the base had triggered memories of some close calls he had had in the past. Not combat danger - he rarely had any dreams about the fighting - it was when his illegal deeds were almost exposed that he felt nervous. Now he sensed a new threat.

Yesterday the Lieutenant had given Bowers an update on the new officers. "Sergeant, the new command team is scheduled to arrive Sunday afternoon. You will organize a platoon review to welcome the new Colonel for Sunday night before evening taps. Then Monday the first wave of National Guard trainees arrives. It's going to be hectic with a thousand new troops pouring in, but most of it won't be our responsibility."

"Yes, sir. Lieutenant, do we know who the new officers are?"

"Yes, Sergeant, the new CO is Colonel Thomas Murphy, the XO is Major Delaney, and there is also a Captain Anderson."

Damn, thought Bowers. The name of Thomas Murphy sounded too familiar. Murphy had been a Lt. Colonel back at Fort Bragg, when he had almost caught up to Ted's enterprises. Bowers had little doubt it was the same man.

At Fort Bragg in Fayetteville, North Carolina, Bowers had run the biggest black market of his life. Bragg was the largest army base in the nation, and with size came opportunities. There were several PX facilities of varying sizes spread over the massive layout. Bowers had cultivated a network of civilian "fences" and paid some of the delivery supply people to look the other way. His operation had gotten too successful and his inner warning alarm had told him he was pushing his luck, but Bowers always had an escape plan.

Every platoon has what Bowers called a "Goober," a naïve, slow kid who was dumb-as-a-post. His "Goober" had been Private Pike. Bowers had used Pike to run some of the errands involving his thefts. Pike was too thick to suspect anything, and the errands put him in positions that would make him look suspicious in an investigation. When Bowers had decided to wrap up his operation, he had played his trump card.

Pike had a girlfriend and he showed everyone her picture. Proud as a peacock, he didn't notice that she had a face that could stop a bullet. The rest of the platoon had made sarcastic jokes about her, but in a way that Pike was too slow to understand. So Bowers played on Pike's gullibility. One day during a barracks inspection he knew Pike had been showing some men the photo.

"Private Pike, let me see that picture."

"Sure thing, Sergeant Bowers."

"Pike, you're a lucky man."

"Thank you, Sergeant. Yessiree, she's a real peach."

"Only one thing, Private."

Pike got that puzzled look. "Gosh, Sergeant, what's that?"

"Well, I'm sure she's real nice, but a girl like that is gonna have every man in your county after her, now that you're gone."

Giggles and snickers spread through the barracks, but Bowers called out, "Attention! I'll have no comments on any soldier's wife or girlfriend. Nothing destroys unit morale more than jealousy or fighting over a woman. Now, Pike is lucky enough to have a pretty girl, and I don't want to hear about anyone making any disparaging comments or teasing him."

He paused and glared across the ranks of men. "Do I make myself clear?"

A ringing chorus shouted, "Yes, Sergeant!"

"Excellent. I just wish all those civilians back home had the same attitude. Pike, you wouldn't be the first soldier who had his sweetheart stolen by some smooth talker."

After Bowers planted that seed, he asked about Pike's girlfriend every chance he got.

"So, Pike, glad your girlfriend is still being faithful. At least I hope she is."

"Yes, Sergeant, far as I know. Why, you think I should be worried?"

"No, Private, I'm sure it'll be fine. Why, you've only got another eighteen months to serve."

Pike's face took on a nervous frown, but Bowers moved along and left him to fret. He also overheard some of the men echoing the same theme. They teased Pike with fake compliments that praised his girlfriend's looks and said they hoped she would be faithful.

When Bowers decided to pull the plug on his operation, he also pulled the plug on Pike. He sent a telegram to Pike and then delivered it to the private himself. It read:

You won't be home for so long - Stop - Chance to marry someone with money - Stop - Don't think I can wait - Stop

"Gosh, Sergeant, what I am I gonna do? I can't lose her, and I ain't got any leave time for another two months."

"Pike, a real man and a real soldier wouldn't let anything stop him from going to her. Pike, you need to step up and be a man."

The next morning, Pike was absent at morning roll call and placed on the AWOL list. When the barracks were empty, Bowers planted the key to the main PX along with some stolen watches in Pike's footlocker. Two days later North Korea invaded South Korea, and Private Pike or any possible PX shortages were forgotten in the scramble to mobilize for combat.

*****

One thing Ted knew: When you had your enemy at a disadvantage, you needed to strike fast. He hated wishy-washy officers who hesitated when they should have pounced. Bowers used the same approach in his personal life. It was Ted against the world. He had no true friends; he didn't trust people and that way they couldn't turn on him or hurt him. If anyone betrayed or harmed him, that person would be the one who got hurt. If he let people get away with one thing, they would think they could do it again. Whether it was in combat or in life, nobody got away with causing Ted Bowers problems.

Now, one of the people who had slipped away from his revenge was within his grasp. The flat tire was just a minor teaser, an irritant to hint at his presence. The next steps would be more painful, and nothing hurt more than endangering the loved one of an enemy. Ted had already done recon and he knew where Curtis lived.

Chapter 12
Rob - Bitter Reflections
Wednesday, 8:00 AM

Rob sipped his second cup of coffee and looked across the low dune and vast beach. The still waters of Cape Cod Bay were deep blue. The rays of the rising sun in the east were just beginning to reflect off the bay waters to the west. It was going to be a beautiful day, but he could feel the rising heat and humidity. Rob subscribed to the old sailors' folklore about the weather: *Red sky at night, sailors' delight. Red sky at morning, sailor take warning.* Last night had cast a red hue and spectacular sunset and predictably, there were no storms in sight. He also believed that the weather on the Cape tended to run in three-to-five-day cycles. If that was true, he figured they were in for a heat wave.

He had awakened in a tangle of sweaty sheets, with a dull headache and a foggy brain from a night of tossing and turning. Rob tried to make sense of why. In most ways, his life was the best it had been since God-knew-when. He was reunited with the love of his life, renovating his beach shack with modern facilities. He had plenty of money, enjoyed his part-time duties as a special police officer, had friends and no real problems. So why did he feel restless?

Rachel's questions about his conversation with Jimmy kept coming to mind. Clearly, she had different expectations. Was it just the difference between men and women, or was that too easy a way to dismiss it? He didn't like to think much about the past, but the bitter truth was that for all his success as an athlete and student, he still felt doubts and fears. You didn't have to be a genius or psychiatrist to understand that being a fatherless-bastard-child had given him a stigma even in the loose social structure of Bound Brook. On top of that, he had a grandfather who had rejected his daughter and her illegitimate baby, a grandfather who was rich and powerful in Bound Brook, and who had refused to even acknowledge the little boy, desperate for a father figure.

His mother had been warm, loving and a free spirit who flouted social conventions. She had refused her father's demand to go away and have the baby in secret. Instead, she had moved in with her younger cousins, Ben and Phyllis Tyler Brown, and had her son. Roberta's mother was a Tyler, and the extended clan had opened their arms, given them a cottage to live in and dared anyone in town to say a bad word about either the mother or child.

It had been natural for the Tylers, who sometimes found themselves at the bottom of the social pecking order of Bound Brook. So Rob had been largely free from shame and lived a happy childhood. He had played with his numerous Tyler cousins and become inseparable friends with Hoopy Hooper and Jimmy Curtis.

And then had come the crushing blow in late August of 1934. His bohemian, artistic mother loved the water. Her new friend was an artist from Provincetown with family money. Rob still remembered him, coming to the cottage all excited. What was his name? He couldn't or wouldn't recall it.

The man had been thrilled over the purchase of his new sailboat. "Roberta, you've got to come try it out with me. I know a man who's designed a new class of sailboat. It's a nineteen-foot, single-mast racer. I've been dying to own one. I paid extra and bought his demonstration model; I think he's going to call it a Lightning. Nobody here has ever seen one. I can't wait to take her out and I want you to come on its maiden voyage. Maybe I can christen it the *Roberta*."

"Do you have room for Rob to join us?"

"Why sure, it carries three for races. He's a strapping boy; it'll be a jolly time. What do you say, boy? Will you join us?"

"No, thank you, sir. Me and the guys got some plans for today."

Rob had ignored his mother's disappointed look. He had never liked this man. He talked funny, using those city words like "jolly" and called him "boy." He wore white linen suits and a straw hat, and he looked at Roberta in a way that made Rob squirm. He knew his mother thought he was fun; she loved adventures and riding in the man's fancy new Rolls-Royce Phantom. His cousins and friends stared whenever the man drove down Tyler Lane to their little cottage. The elegant automobile looked completely out of place on the oyster-shell driveway.

"Wow, can you believe that car? It musta cost a fortune," said a gawking Hoopy. "You think he's a millionaire, Rob?"

"I heard somebody say his family is from Philadelphia and they got more money than Carnegie or Rockefeller," Jimmy chimed in.

Rob didn't much care, but his mother seemed happy.

He knew he should have gone sailing. Maybe another set of hands would have kept the sailboat under control when a sudden, wild storm came from nowhere. Some people claim they saw a swirling water spout, a water tornado. Gale force winds had raged, and a torrential downpour had drenched Rob and his friends on their daily trek across the mudflats. Then in less than thirty minutes it was over, thirty minutes that changed his life. The capsized boat had been towed into the harbor hours later, but it had taken two days before fishermen spotted the bodies, washed up in the weeds near the entrance to the Bound Brook Gut.

Rob was not the only person to suffer loss; it was common in Bound Brook. The hard life on the waters often ended in tragedy. Jimmy Curtis had lost his father at sea when he was in high school. Then World War II had added to the funerals and too-young deaths of Bound Brook men. Rob had served in the Navy, first as a shipping clerk in Newport, where he also played for the base's basketball team. Then he had been transferred to the Navy Shore Patrol in Marseille, France. He had been in the war, but mostly away from the action, unlike Jimmy Curtis, Hoopy and many others from town. Later in life, his loss had been more emotional: the loss of his true love Rachel, the betrayal by his best friend Jimmy . . . and then there was Marie LaVache.

When the war ended, Rob had been scheduled to return home to be mustered out of the Navy. It would have meant the end of the romance. A tearful Marie had pleaded with him to come back to France, and her doting father had made him an offer. LaVache proposed Rob work for him, using his knowledge of shipping procedures. To sweeten the deal LaVache had given him a huge bonus and a generous salary. Naïvely, Rob was lost in love and feeling there was nothing back home for him. He was fascinated by the world of business in the bustling port of Marseille. He was glad to share his information about Navy shipping and never realized that he was being used.

Then one day a person's casual remark sparked recognition. Sometimes he felt so stupid when what should be obvious smacked him in the face. How did a French businessman survive in Vichy France, that was run by the Nazis? Rob had heard about collaborators before, but this was new to him. Why wasn't LaVache punished like the other turncoats?

The answer seemed to be that Emile's shipping empire was too big and he was too crafty. He knew how to play both sides, and all the governments needed his resources and fleet of ships. Now LaVache had found more money doing illegal shipping, the black market, that flourished during and right after the war. What better help in avoiding detection than a navy expert in shipping procedures, documents and schedules? It helped that his daughter loved Rob, but it was secondary to Emile's purposes.

What had followed was a shouting match. Betrayed and hurt, Rob had no idea what he was facing. After screaming at LaVache and enduring Marie's tears, Rob barely remembered what had happened next. He did remember being grabbed by Emile's burly bodyguards, some heavy punches and then it all went black. When he regained consciousness, every part of his body ached and his face was swollen like a balloon. All he had was a wad of cash and a note that read, "Don't come back. Don't ever try to see her."

Rob now shook his head, and a thought jumped into his brain. He was so stupid. Did he think that just because Rachel was divorcing Jimmy and they were back together that it was suddenly 1940, and he was eighteen again? A lot had happened in twelve years. Was he ready for a mature relationship? Could he open his damaged soul to a deep emotional bond? Was this what Rachel was hinting at?

This was uncharted territory for him and he was uncomfortable. No more cocoon, no more meandering through life. Rachel deserved commitment and effort. He couldn't give her more years of being just like Jimmy. He didn't know how to do it, but being aware was a start. It ran the risk of being hurt again, but wasn't that life? He knew he wanted to try.

*****

A ringing sound interrupted his thoughts: the telephone. It had only been a week and he wasn't used to the jarring sound from the instrument he had installed in his cottage. Modern conveniences had their disadvantages. He picked up on the fourth ring.

"Hello?"

"Hi, Rob. It's Diane Ellis. Chief Foster says he needs you to work on Friday the Fourth and the whole weekend. After that, he says you can have the summer off if you need it. He's got enough summer help to get by."

"Thanks, Diane. What hours?"

"For now you can work the day shifts, but he says be ready for overtime if the weekend gets crazy."

"Tell the Chief I'll be there." He hung up, but rested his hand on the phone receiver. Diane was the day dispatcher for the Police and Fire Departments. Bill "Bull" Foster was the Police Chief, a position he had taken after retiring from the Massachusetts State Police. Bull had earned his nickname for his formidable size and his dogged determination. Rob had rarely met anyone who made him feel small, but Foster was a mountain of a man.

Another jarring ring and vibration made him jump. He now began to doubt his decision to install the phone. *What now?* "Hello?"

"Hey, Rob. It's Hoopy. You okay?"

"Sorry to be so gruff, still getting used to this phone interrupting my day."

"Are you working on Friday afternoon? We've got the annual baseball game against Wellfleet, and I'm having trouble rounding up a full team. Many of the usual guys are working on the Fourth. With all the tourists, lots of businesses are staying open."

"Sorry, the Chief needs me the whole weekend. Did you talk to George about recruiting players?"

"Yes, talked to him last night. Rachel is going to play, and George said he'll talk to Jimmy about umpiring. George says he'd like to play, but Maggie would probably kill him. He suggested he might be able to get some soldiers from Camp Wellfleet to fill out the team if we get stuck."

"Well, good luck. Wish I could play, but duty calls."

Chapter 13
Ted - Burning Revenge
Wednesday Morning

"I have done a thousand dreadful things
As willingly as one would kill a fly,
And nothing grieves me heartily indeed
But that I cannot do ten thousand more."
William Shakespeare - Titus Andronicus: Act 5, Scene 1

George, Benny and Jim had made great progress setting up the store. Shelves were stocked with enough products to open on Monday, back stock was moved to the storage area and today the cash registers had been delivered. Good thing because Thursday was their last chance to work before the holiday. George was setting up the cash registers in three locations when Simon arrived around 10:00. He had a large foam brace around his neck and walked with a cane.

"Gee, Simon, are you alright? I didn't expect you back so soon."

"The garage let me borrow a car while they fix my fender, tire and the alignment. I still ache all over, got a huge bruise on my knee and my neck is stiff. Doctor said it might be a week before I'm back to normal. Meanwhile I'm good enough to check on things. Actually, I have to say, the store looks pretty good, George."

George suppressed his surprise. "Thanks, Simon. Benny and Jim are great workers. Listen; there is something I need to talk to you about."

Simon frowned. "If you are looking for overtime, don't even think about it."

"No, I think we have a problem, but I can't put a finger on it. I swear we are missing some of our cartons of products. Most of them are cigarettes. I checked with Ben and Jim and they noticed it too. I looked back on the delivery slips and checked it against the inventory. The slips and inventory agree, but something is fishy. Based on my memory I know the stacks of cigarettes are short one each. It's hard to see, and the delivery slips look like they have been doctored."

Simon looked like he had seen a ghost. "How could that be? Did Ben or Jim steal them? I thought you said we could trust them."

"I'll vouch for both of them, and I know I didn't take any. None of us even smokes. Do you and I have the only keys? I am here every morning before the guys arrive, and I lock up after they leave. It's not us."

"You said the delivery slips and inventory agree, right? So you must be mistaken."

"Look, Simon, I can't prove it, but I swear we are missing at least five full boxes of cigarettes and a box of wristwatches."

Simon's shoulders slumped. "What do we do?"

"My suggestion is that we make a written record of our suspicions and after we sign for any new deliveries we should lock and hide the delivery slips. When we get a visit from the company representative, we can explain what we suspect and how we have been handling it. I also think we should have the locks changed. I know a locksmith in Orleans. I already called him and asked him to come over. If you give your approval, he'll change the locks tomorrow."

"George, I've never handled anything like this. I need your help. Do whatever you think is right and I'll approve it."

"Simon, I'll take care of it."

"Thanks, George. You know, I have to admit something to you. I grew up in a store, but I was never good at it. I'm going to need all the help I can get. I feel I can trust you. I hope you don't think I'm stupid or weak."

"Just the opposite, Simon. It's a strong man who can ask for help when he needs it."

"That makes me feel better, George. So, tell me what needs to be done."

*****

With all four men working, the store took shape. Simon felt a relief to have George directing the work. For the first time in his life, he just did the tasks that needed to be completed, without worrying that his father was judging him.

In another first for Simon, he decided to take decisive action. The words of his father echoed in his memory: *Nobody steals from an Eldredge.* Before closing time, he told George his plan. When the other three left, he locked the doors and started the old Ford the garage folks had let him borrow. Simon drove out the gate and nodded to the guard, who waved him ahead. A hundred yards down Route 6, he pulled over off to the side.

He walked back to the base and stopped at the guardhouse when the soldier on duty put up his hand and asked his business. "Hi, remember me? I'm Simon Eldredge, I manage the PX. I had some car trouble, so I need to go back to the base and use a phone. I'll call someone to pick me up and have them meet me out on the highway. I might do a little more work in the PX first, so it could be a while."

After he was signed back in, he walked toward the PX and found a good spot to hide in a thicket of bushes. He sat down and waited. His neck started to kill him, and he wished he had taken more aspirin. He was almost ready to give up, when a figure approached the back door. In the dim light, he couldn't make out the face, but he was dressed in regular clothes. The person fiddled with the door and then it opened. In less than fifteen minutes, the door opened from the inside and the intruder stepped out, locked the door and left. By now, it was too dark to do more than see a dim outline and impossible to see where the thief had headed.

*****

Ted had decided he would wrap up his PX thefts tonight. With the new CO taking command this weekend, Bowers would be pushing his luck. Colonel Murphy might remember him from Fort Bragg. If he were a prudent man, Ted would have called it quits already. But there was something about taking his chances, and even more about deceiving authority, manipulating the system and pulling the wool over officers' eyes. It wasn't a thrill without taking the risk.

Tonight would be the end. After all, he had a more important mission. He wasn't done with his revenge against Curtis. Tonight would be the next step as he escalated the pressure. Before he was done, Curtis would wish he was back in Korea.

After taps and the lowering of the flag, Bowers changed into civilian clothes, went out the back of his quarters and took a roundabout route to the rear of the PX. Once inside, he perused the shelves. The store looked almost ready to open. He looked around for the delivery packing slips, but they seemed to have been stored away somewhere. It was obvious that he couldn't steal entire boxes of items anymore.

He contented himself with stealing individual objects from the back of the display rows: a few watches (Timex and

Bulova); individual packs of cigarettes (mostly Marlboros, his personal favorite). He just took things he could stick in his pockets. Oh well, it had been good while it lasted, but this was the end.

Ted locked the door and headed for the thick woods at the edge of the base. He followed a narrow path through the deep brush until it connected to the remains of a rutted dirt road. Barely more than a cart path, the beginnings of small shrubs and trees poked through the soil. He followed the road until it widened and showed signs of tire tracks.

In the dim twilight, he saw his landmark and turned back into the woods where an ancient hardwood tree had split near its base. The left trunk rose up about five feet before it grew off to the side toward the southeast following the path of the day's sunlight. Its overhanging limbs cast shade over a bare patch of ground that provided just enough room to park a car.

In May, Bowers had spotted the 1941 Chevy Convertible with a hand lettered For Sale sign on a back road in South Wellfleet. The body was in tough shape and the cloth top had several rips. The tires were almost bald and the driver's side was missing the handle to roll down the window. The upholstery was torn and looked like it provided homes for various wildlife. However, when the old man who owned it had started the engine, it leapt to life with a strong roar. Ted had taken it for a short drive and found several gauges didn't work, the steering was stiff and it pulled to the right. Nevertheless, the price was cheap, and the old man seemed glad to get rid of it.

Ted had gotten Private Henderson to drop him off after they had made a food supply run into Wellfleet. He had the Private leave him at the entrance to the old man's road, and told Henderson he would get a ride back. Ted didn't want anyone to see the car, or even know he had one. He was sure it violated several regulations.

He had stashed the car down this old dirt road under the spreading tree and covered it with branches and leaves. It still had the old license plate, although the registration had expired. Ted always made contingency plans. He hadn't known how or even if he would use the car, but it was so cheap he could afford to abandon it without a second thought. So far, it had just been a place to hide his stolen goods. Now it was going to pay off. Tonight, he didn't want anyone seeing an army Jeep.

He uncovered the car, stuck his pilfered merchandise under the front seat, started it up and switched on the headlights. It was less than a few hundred yards to the highway, and Ted pulled out onto a deserted Route 6 about a half mile from the Camp Wellfleet entrance. He kept the old heap at what he hoped was the speed limit. He couldn't tell for sure, since the gauge didn't work. The last thing he wanted was to be pulled over by some local cop.

Ted rolled along Route 6, through Wellfleet and into the village of Bound Brook. He found the left turn to Herring Brook Road and followed along a twisty lane until he came to a driveway and a sign that read *Curtis*. Halfway down the driveway was a wide area, a turnaround. He parked his old car facing out toward the road and as far off to the side as he dared, then rummaged in the back seat and pulled out a gas can.

He flicked on a flashlight that he kept pointed at the ground as he walked the remaining fifty yards to the Curtis house. Around a bend in the road, he saw a building with lights twinkling from the windows. The house was a shingled style, probably what they called a Cape, an appropriate name. Ted wasn't interested in the house. On his scouting mission, he had found his target. There was a separate building, perhaps an old garage or storage shed, twenty yards from the main house. He saw Curtis' Chrysler parked in front. Perfect, it meant he and his mother were home.

Bowers had no qualms about killing Curtis or even his mother. However, he didn't want the investigation that it would bring. Burning down the old shack might be scary, but not fatal. Anything could have started it, maybe just kids sneaking a cigarette. He crept to the side of the garage, knelt down and brushed some pine needles and leaves against the side of the wooden building. Opening the can, he splashed gasoline on the side of the building, then on the leaves. He scraped together a short trail of leaves and needles, only about a foot long, and sprinkled more gasoline.

Finally, he made another leaf pile connecting the trail to the garage, poured a heavier dose of the combustible liquid and screwed the cap back on. He pulled out a pack of Marlboros, put one in his mouth, flicked open his army lighter and sucked in a deep pull of breath as he lit the tip. He shook out the remaining half-dozen cigarettes and scattered them around, then crushed the empty package and dropped it on the driveway in plain view. He took several puffs and watched the cigarette give off a bright red glow. Then he bent down and stood the cigarette on its unlit end into the mound of soaked leaves, with less than an inch between the burning end and the flammable stack.

Ted grabbed the gas can and double-timed back to his car. He stumbled over a hidden root and the gas can tumbled from his grip. Suppressing a curse, he scooped up the almost empty can and ran to his car. He pulled out of the driveway, looked over his shoulder and waited. A spark of light burst the night darkness; he smirked, then turned onto Herring Brook Road.

He drove on backroads until he got into Wellfleet. He did not want to be observed by the fire trucks or police cars as they rushed to the scene. As if on cue, the blast of a siren screamed through the night. There were several blasts, indicating some location code he guessed. Then a pause and the blasts started again.

Chapter 14
Jim - Cellar Savers
Wednesday Night

Jim had parked the Packard in the parking lot of Art's Bar and Grill on Bound Brook Harbor. A few minutes later he was sitting on a stool between Honk Snow and Bunky Morris. He hadn't been out to a bar since he had returned to Bound Brook. When he had lived in town between the wars, he had practically lived at Art's. But when he got home from Korea, he had known that liquor and bars were not his friends. Besides, it felt good to stay in at his mother's house and let her cook and fuss over him.

What was he doing here? Deep down he knew it was a mistake. Maybe talking with George and Rob had brought up some of his old demons. When he walked in, Bunky called out to everyone. "Hey, let me have your attention. I want you all to welcome home Bound Brook's hero. I want to be the first to buy this man a beer."

The dozen or so patrons stood and gave him a round of applause. "And I'll be the second," echoed Honk.

So now here he sat, trying to nurse his third Gansett while dodging questions about what it was like to be fighting in Korea.

Then everyone heard the sound and the bar went silent. The fire siren blasted out its code. Bunky, Honk and half the bar jumped up and ran for the door.

"Jimmy, you coming?" Bunky shouted. "That's three blasts, your end of town. Let's go!"

Jimmy followed the crowd out the door. He started his new Packard and joined the parade of cars heading toward Herring Brook. Almost every male over the age of sixteen belonged to the Bound Brook Volunteer Fire Department. The fire and police shared one building. The police department was on the top floor; two fire engines, behind the double bay doors, were located at ground level. One member always stayed in the fire station.

When a fire was reported, the dispatcher gave them the exact location, and that person started the first engine and raced to the fire with lights flashing and siren blaring. One or two others who lived nearby rushed to the station to get the second truck. The rest of the members drove in the general direction of the fire and watched for smoke, flames or the siren of the police cruiser or fire truck.

The rural geography made it hard to save many houses. With only one fire station and just two engines, it took too long to get to most fires. It was the reason that volunteer fire departments were derisively dubbed "Cellar Savers." However, everyone took the responsibility seriously and when it came to brush or forest fires, they were all that prevented large sections of the town from going up in flames.

Jim could see a light in the night sky. He felt a chill and then a stunned realization. They were going to his house.

*****

An hour later, fire hoses sprayed water on a smoking pile of rubble. Jim comforted his mother until her best friend, Maggie Gilmore, arrived on the scene. The two women sat on the running board of Engine #2 with Maggie's arm draped around Mabel's shoulders. Fortunately the fire had been contained to the old garage, but the dry wood had gone up like matchsticks. Crews from neighboring Wellfleet had joined the effort, the firemen focusing their attention on wetting the surrounding trees and Mabel's house, while soaking the dilapidated shack.

Fire Chief Buddy Barrows directed others to knock down the building as fast as possible. The quicker they could get it to the ground, the sooner it would not pose a threat. Now a murky haze, the smell of smoke and the sticky feel of dampness were all that remained.

With the fire under control, Chief Barrows huddled with Police Chief Foster, Special Officers Rob Caldwell and Skip Parker, and their counterparts from Wellfleet, Police Chief Bill Fleming, Fire Chief Lester Taylor and Assistant Charlie Huntley. Jimmy joined them and caught part of the conversation.

Foster was speaking. "Mabel said she heard a noise, a clunking sound, like a metal barrel or something, so she looked out the kitchen window. She didn't see anything in the dark, but suddenly the whole side of the garage went up in flames."

"We found some cigarettes and an empty Marlboro pack near the garage." said Skip Parker. "Coulda been kids sneaking a smoke."

Foster motioned toward Curtis. "Here's Jim, let's ask him what was in the garage."

"Hi, Guys. Thanks for taking care of my mother and protecting the house from catching fire. You want to know what was in the old garage? Well, almost nothing. My mother had everything cleaned out, way back when my father died. I used the house basement for my workshop and we didn't even put the car in the garage. It didn't have a proper car door that worked anyway."

"Were there flammable liquids, gasoline, kerosene or anything like that?" asked Barrows. "Maybe old rags or clothes that were soaked with grease?"

"No, Buddy. There was an old workbench and some pegboards on the walls, but we didn't keep tools or anything in there anymore. Probably should have torn it down years ago. Just never got around to it."

Chief Fleming, another retired State Trooper, spoke up. "Bull, it sounds suspicious; Mrs. Curtis' description of the sudden bursting of flames doesn't sound accidental. Of course, I suppose kids could have tossed a cigarette or match into some leaves. It smoldered and then caught the dry leaves on fire."

Fleming looked at Jim. "You had any trouble with kids hanging around the property? Any neighbors we should talk with?"

"Not that I know of. You can ask George if there are any school-age kids around here, but our nearest neighbor is half a mile away and they're elderly."

"I wish I knew what that clunking sound was that Mabel heard," said Chief Foster. "Makes me think somebody was out here. Most likely kids, sharing cigarettes they stole out of their house. The thing is we have a suspicious fire to a worthless building and no harm to the house, car or anything of value. Arson is a crime, but it is damned hard to prove, and the DA isn't interested in cases where nobody was hurt and nothing was harmed."

Skip looked around. "Reminds me of the Proctor fire from last winter, but in that case we had a dead body. And I guess we know who set that one."

Jim had still been in Korea, but he had heard about the death of Old Man Proctor. Rob had been instrumental in solving the case. Unfortunately, it had a tragic ending that still left people in town shaken.

"I hope we don't have a fire bug," Barrows added.

The group separated and went off to their responsibilities. Jim saw Rachel and George and went over to talk with them.

George looked up. "Jim, your mother is going to spend the night at our house. I think this whole thing has made her too upset to be here tonight. What about you? Do you need a place to stay?"

"No, I'll sleep here and keep an eye on things."

Rob joined the group. "Chief says things are under control. Skip is on patrol tonight, and he is going to swing by every hour or so to check on things and make sure the fire doesn't restart."

Others nodded agreement.

"Rob, can we talk a minute?" asked Rachel.

George and Jim took the hint and walked away.

"Mabel is going to stay at our house, and I want her to sleep in my bed. Do you happen to know somewhere I can spend the night?"

"Hmm . . . That's a hard question, let me think. The boarding house might have a room. . . ." Rachel kicked his shin. "Ouch! Oh wait a minute, I might have room."

"Mister, you are in serious trouble. You better make it up to me."

"Well, we'll see what I can do."

Chapter 15
Simon – Taking Charge
Thursday, July 3rd

Simon woke at the crack-of-dawn. He could not remember when he had been so excited. It was like, after years of being the baby brother and constant screw-up, he had grown up overnight. George's patience and respect was a big part of it. The older man didn't seem to judge him, like everyone in his life had always done. It had been the catalyst to his stakeout last night. For once, he felt like he was taking charge. He treated himself to a breakfast at Agnes' Restaurant in the center of Bound Brook.

It was 7:00 but there was a crowd of locals and a buzz of energy in the air. "Well, that was a lucky fire last night. If Mabel hadn't been home and called right away, the house and brush would have gone up in flames. Instead of just putting out an old garage, we could have had a major forest fire."

"Yeah, Bunky. I heard Wellfleet was called in to help."

"Yup, Moose, just a precaution. Buddy said he wanted them already on the scene in case it spread to the woods and marsh. You should have been there; we missed you."

"Well, some of us got two jobs. I had to work at the Mayflower last night. We didn't hear the siren out in Provincetown, and couldn't have left if we had. Starting to get lots of tourists with the holiday tomorrow."

Simon summoned up his courage. "Excuse me, where was the fire?"

"Old garage, out at the Curtis place in the Herring Brook area. Hey, ain't you the guy that works at the PX?"

"Yes, I am. Would that be Jim Curtis' place?"

"Yup," continued Bunky. "He wasn't home. He was with me and Honk at Art's, but his mother saw the garage go up in flames and called before it spread."

"So, nobody hurt, I hope."

"No. Mabel sure was shook up though. Can't say I blame her. Fire is a scary thing."

"Hey, changing the subject," said Moose, "Any of you guys playing in the baseball game tomorrow? I know us highway-crew guys are gonna be tied up cleaning up after the parade."

"I heard some of the younger guys and high school kids are playing. Benny Brown, Bobby Snow, Vinnie Costa, a few others maybe. Hey here's Buddy. You playing in the game?"

"Hi, Bunky. Yup, I am. Me, Hoopy, Ben Sr. and I heard that Rachel was going to play. George says he'll try to get some soldiers from Camp Wellfleet to fill spots for either team."

That caught Simon's attention. "Excuse me, a woman is going to play baseball with you men?"

Moose laughed. "Yes, she is, and not your average woman. Rachel might be small, but she is probably better than half the guys in the game. She's George's daughter, you know, and I guess he was a real star athlete back in his day. Must be in the blood."

The group of men went back to their conversation. Simon thought about what he had heard. Only recently had he learned that Curtis was a war hero, and about his divorce. Benny had told him when Simon asked about the limp and missing fingers. Jim was sure having a string of bad luck. He had two flat tires, a garage fire, a divorce . . . and all that on top of his war wounds. Curtis must have been made of tough stuff. Simon thought how his father, Chandler Eldredge, would have commented on Jim's grit while giving Simon a dirty look.

Well, maybe Simon could make his father proud after all. *Nobody steals from an Eldredge.*

*****

George pulled into the PX around 8:15 and was surprised to see Simon's borrowed car already there. In fact, Simon was at the back door, watching the driver unload a delivery truck. While George parked, Simon signed off on the delivery paper work. The neck brace and cane were gone.

"Hi, George. We'll have to do some rearranging. Just got a big delivery of sports equipment. I completely forgot that we needed a section for that stuff. But, don't worry, I already figured out where we can put all of it."

George was surprised. This did not sound like the Simon he knew.

"Hi, Simon. Sounds like you got it under control. Tell me where you want to put it and I'll get started. The guys should be here soon."

"Okay, George, but first I need to tell you about what I saw last night." He told George all the details of his snooping.

"So, Simon, it was either a soldier in civilian clothes, or somebody who snuck onto the base. But you said he had a key?"

"Yes, definitely had a key. Good thing we're getting the locks changed today. I think I need to report it to the officer in charge of the base. You think I should?"

"Absolutely. You want me to come with you?"

"Well, I guess you better watch the store until the other guys get here. I can take care of it."

Simon walked the paved main road of the base to the building with a flag and the sign *Command Post.* Inside was a soldier behind a counter.

"May I help you, sir?"

"Yes, I'm the PX manager and I need to speak with your commanding officer."

"That would be Lieutenant Gallant. I'll get him for you." The soldier disappeared into an office.

"Hello, I'm Lieutenant Gallant. I am in temporary command of the base. How may I help you?"

"Lieutenant, my name is Simon Eldredge. I manage the PX. I need to tell you about our stolen inventory and what I saw last night."

He told Gallant the whole story. When he got to the part about the night before, the Lieutenant's brow wrinkled in a frown.

"Are you sure the person had a key? You didn't forget to lock it up, did you?" Simon made a face and shook his head. "No, of course you didn't. Sorry, just thinking aloud. So how can I help?"

"We are getting the locks changed today, so it shouldn't be a problem anymore. However, before we got the keys, I believe it was from your Captain. Who else had them, and how many were there?"

"Unfortunately, all the other officers have shipped out overseas, so I can't answer. The only remaining people in any position of command are the Sergeant and myself." The Lieutenant turned around. "Private, would you get the Sergeant for me?"

"Yes, sir. I believe that's him now."

A good-looking rugged soldier came through the door. "Sergeant, just in time."

"Yes, sir. What do you need?"

"Mr. Eldredge is the PX manager. Last night he saw someone use a key to get into the PX. They've had stuff stolen. Do you know anyone who has a key to the store?"

Ted paused. "Hmm . . . no, sir. I think Corporal Wagner had the keys first. Then he gave them to me and I passed them on to the Captain right away. There were only two as far as I know."

"Okay, thank you, Sergeant. Keep your eyes open and check with the Corporal."

"I will, sir. I'll let you know if I learn anything."

"Mr. Eldredge is having the locks changed today, so it shouldn't be a problem anymore, but I'd like to find out if we have a thief in our platoon."

"Yes, sir, most likely one of the civilian contractors. I expect some of them would know how to pick a lock."

"Good point, Sergeant. I hadn't thought of that."

Simon nodded. "Yes, I suppose with all the builders around, it could be one of them. Anyway, thank you for your help, Lieutenant."

"You are welcome. I'll keep you posted."

"Oh before I go, you might be interested to know that we just got a shipment of sports equipment. Lots of baseball stuff: balls, gloves, some nice Louisville Slugger bats; also a few footballs and basketballs. I thought you might want to buy some equipment for the men to play sports in their free time."

"Thank you, Mr. Eldredge. I'll make sure to tell the new CO when he gets settled after Sunday."

Simon smiled, pleased with himself. His father would like that. Always take an opportunity to push your products when you talk with a likely customer.

*****

When Simon got back to the PX, he pitched in with setting up the store. By the end of the day, it looked ready for business.

"Simon, I think we are set to go."

"Yes, George, I think you're right. All the shelves are stocked, extra inventory stowed away, cash registers ready, opening cash for change locked away . . . Yup, I think we're set for Monday."

"I trained Jim and Benny on running the cash register. They've both worked in stores before, so they know how to make change and ring up sales. Do you have a sense of when the soldiers will be buying things? Is there a schedule?"

Simon nodded. "Yes, we won't get overrun by a thousand National Guard all at once. They'll have a schedule of when they can have PX visits, and it will be spread out one company or platoon at a time."

"That's a relief," chuckled George.

"Well, I want to talk to all three of you. Jim . . . Ben . . . Can you come over here?"

Jim looked up from dusting a counter. "Sure, Simon. What's up?"

Simon looked at all three. "I want to tell you all what a great job you've done getting the store set up. I know I wasn't much help." He paused. "Not just the accident, it's just, well, I've never been a manager before, and I didn't know what to do, and well, I guess I didn't want to admit it. But now, well, I know I can count on you three, and I think I can do a better job of pulling my own weight."

After an awkward silence, George spoke. "Simon, you'll do fine. Let's work together and maybe we can have some fun in the process. Right, guys?"

Jim and Ben nodded their agreement.

Simon laughed. "Yes, I think it can be fun. You guys have a good Fourth of July weekend and I'll see you Monday."

Chapter 16
Rachel & Rob – The Talk
Thursday Morning

Rachel heard the sound of dishes rattling and sniffed the smell of coffee even before she opened her eyes. She rolled over and looked around the knotty pine walls of Rob's small bedroom. It wasn't her bedroom at home, but it was comfortable. She threw back the covers, stood up, stretched and grabbed one of his oversized undershirts.

"Hey, do I hear something stirring around in there?"

"Just me, and I'm ravenous."

"Sounds like someone else worked up an appetite from last night."

"You could say that, but first I need coffee."

"Help yourself to the coffee and scrambled eggs. I'll have pancakes ready in a jiffy. You want any toast?"

"No, eggs and pancakes should be plenty." She poured a mug of coffee and dished some eggs onto a chipped plate. She helped herself to the milk and sugar on the table and took a deep drink of the coffee. "Okay, that hits the spot."

Rob ladled pancake batter onto a griddle. He turned and gave her a wink. "I'd give you a kiss too, but I don't want to get you all excited again."

"Excited," laughed Rachel,."Look who's talking."

"Well, maybe it is me that I don't trust."

She watched him flip the pancakes. For a moment, she saw the teenage boy she had fallen in love with, and wondered about all the lost years in between. Now he was a grown man, confident and handsome, and she was a mature woman. It was just that twelve-year gap in between.

Rob dished the pancakes onto a platter and placed them on the table. "Here you go, m'lady. Butter and syrup are on the table. You okay? You suddenly look so serious."

"No, I'm fine. Just thinking."

He sat down, spread butter and then poured syrup on his pancakes. "Well, I've been thinking too."

"Oh, I think I know what you've been thinking about."

"Well, that too, but seriously, some of the things you've said rang true."

"Really, and what would those things be?"

"Maybe it's not so much what you said; more like what you didn't say. It got me thinking about the way I handle my feelings."

"Wow, a man talking about his feelings. I'm shocked."

Rob smiled. "I know, it is a little strange isn't it, but hear me out. When my mother died, I was devastated. I finally snapped out of it with a combination of basketball, your father, Hoopy, Jimmy and you. You became the most important person in my life. Then I lost you, and it was like starting over again, like when my mother died."

Rachel reached over and touched his hand. "I'm sorry."

"I know. Me too, but let me finish. It's hard, but I've got to get it out. After, well . . . after you and Jimmy got married, I still had college and basketball, but I didn't have anyone significant in my life anymore. I understand now that I put up emotional walls. I went through life, worked and played hard, but I shut down my feelings and didn't let anybody in. I didn't want to let anyone in; you know, if you don't let people in, then you can't get hurt."

"What about when you were in France and you fell for Marie?"

"That was different. I think now it was an infatuation, more like a schoolboy crush. Marie was very young; I was older and an American. She wanted me, and it was hard to resist her. I was lonely, she was pretty and the possibilities were intriguing. We definitely had a relationship, and it was fun while it lasted, but it wasn't deeply committed. We never talked about anything serious. Maybe I let down my barriers a little bit, I'm not sure. The way it ended, though, well, that made me feel I should never let anyone in again."

"I can understand that. It makes complete sense."

"Yes, but now I realize I still have kept those barriers up. I know we are back together and . . . don't get me wrong, it's great! Somehow, though, I think I want it to be like we were still eighteen and just graduated. But we are older and time has passed. I know now that I have some work to do, that life isn't that simple. I sense you have been trying get something across to me, maybe that was it."

Rachel couldn't reply. She just nodded.

"I want to make a real commitment. We aren't the same people we were twelve years ago. I think we need to grow, and learn to love each other as the people we have become, even if we have to deal with all the baggage and hurt feelings. I've been afraid for years and I'm tired of it. I want this to work and I'm willing to risk the pain. It's just . . . Well, I know I loved the young Rachel, and now I want to get to know Rachel, the woman. I know I can love her too, but I need to open up."

Rachel wiped a tear from her cheek. "That is the most touching thing I've ever heard." She stood up so fast that her coffee spilled. Ignoring that, she grabbed his hand, pulled him to his feet and threw herself into his arms. Her kisses covered his face. "I love you. Yes, we need to talk, but there is plenty of time. First, I want to do something else . . . again."

She took his arm and led him to the bedroom.

*****

Jim Curtis kicked off his shoes and stripped off his shirt. He went to the refrigerator and took out the carton of milk. It had been a long day, but now he had three days off. He sipped from the milk container and chuckled to himself. Good thing his mother wasn't home or he'd be in big trouble. He could hear her now. "James Curtis, were you raised by wolves? Get a glass and drink like a civilized person."

Tomorrow was the parade and the annual baseball game. When he was a kid, the Fourth had been his favorite holiday . . . Okay, maybe Christmas was better because he got presents. He was usually walking in the parade with the boy scouts or riding on a float. Now he felt like an outsider, just another spectator.

Mabel had left a note that she was going to spend a few more nights at the Gilmore house. He didn't want to sit in the house alone. If someone had wanted to burn down the house, they wouldn't have set the garage on fire. Last night had rekindled an itch that he knew he shouldn't scratch. Liquor had never done him any good, but he felt an urge and was too weak to resist.

Not Art's though, he didn't want to be the war hero. He needed some place where people didn't know his life story. He put on his shoes and a clean t-shirt, and headed out the door to Provincetown.

He stumbled back home around midnight and just managed to kick off his shoes before he tumbled onto the couch. It was almost 10:00 before he opened his eyes. Well, guess he wasn't going to the parade.

He rolled off the couch and went to the bathroom. When he finished, he took two aspirin and washed them down with a handful of tap water. Then he realized, for the first time in years he hadn't woken up at dawn. More surprising: he hadn't had the dream.

Chapter 17
Jim - The Game Within The Game
Friday, July 4th

Cars started to arrive at Wellfleet's Mayo Beach field around 1:30 for the traditional rivalry baseball game between Bound Brook and Wellfleet. Jimmy pulled his Packard beside several familiar pickups, sedans and coupes. A few players were already playing catch and stretching. He headed over to the visitors' side bench, where he saw Hoopy. "Hi, Hoop. Do you still need an umpire?"

"Sure do. The new Wellfleet Principal, Dick Cochran, is going to do the bases, but if you would ump the plate that would be great. We're playing six innings, so I'm thinking you two can switch after three, so everyone will feel it's fair."

"Sounds good. Hopefully my gimpy knee won't be a problem."

Jimmy spotted some familiar faces from Wellfleet; Ken Rose, Kenny Snow and Paul Lussier were men who had played basketball against Bound Brook back when Jimmy, Hoopy and Rob had been league champions. Ernie Tesson, Don Gross and Eddie Maker he recognized from the more recent Wellfleet High School Teams, and Lenny Pierce was experienced and had a reputation as a crafty pitcher. Joe Pellegrino, married to one of the Taylor girls, gave him a wave. Jim figured that Wellfleet would field a formidable team.

The Bound Brook players were playing catch, and he saw a mix of young high school players and a few his age. The young guys—Bobby Snow, Vinnie Costa and Benny Brown Jr.—had played for Bound Brook's basketball team. Benny was on the sideline, pitching to his father, Ben Sr. who was wearing catcher's gear. He saw Rachel playing catch with Buddy

Barrows as Hoopy and George Gilmore watched. Seeing Rachel with the guys didn't surprise Jimmy; everyone in town knew she could more than hold her own with the men.

An army Jeep pulled up and two men jumped out, while the driver drove to the end of the line of cars. Hoopy walked over to greet the two soldiers. "Hi, guys. Thanks for coming. We can sure use a few extra players. Just call me Hoopy. I pulled together the Bound Brook team. We're a couple of players short, and Wellfleet could probably use one more."

"I'm Private Joe Ramsdell and this is Private Calvin Dalby. We both played in high school. You can play us anywhere, but we played outfield the most. I think we can hold our own. The Sarge will be here in a minute."

"Great, why don't you join our team and tell your Sergeant he can play for Wellfleet. I think we are going to need all the help we can get."

Jimmy listened in as Hoopy called the Bound Brook players together to go over the lineup and batting order. "Okay, looks like we have just nine players. Joey Pierce and Jerry Paine hope to make it later, and I'll put them as subs. Wellfleet is the home team, so we're up first.

"Here is the lineup: Buddy is at third, leading off; Private Dalby is in left field, batting second; Private Ramsdell in center, hitting third; Bobby at first, hitting cleanup; Ben Sr. is catching and batting fifth; Benny's pitching and sixth; I'm at shortstop, hitting seventh; Vinnie in right, batting eighth; and Rachel at second base, in the ninth spot. George is helping me coach, and he'll keep track of the batting order."

Wellfleet finished their team meeting and took the field. Jimmy grabbed the umpire mask and chest protector and headed to the plate, where Ed Maker was crouched, warming up Lenny Pierce. Jimmy bent over, to practice eyeing the pitches and to test his knee. He thought he could manage three innings. Lenny was smacking the ball into Eddie's mitt and Jim was feeling glad he wasn't playing. "Last one," said Ed as he caught the ball and pegged a practice throw to second base.

"Play ball!" yelled Jimmy.

Buddy Barrows tapped his bat on the plate and squinted at the pitcher. Lenny wound up and fired a pitch, but Buddy squared and dropped a perfect bunt down the third base line. He scampered to first before Kenny Snow could field it cleanly.

That was the last hit for Bound Brook in the inning. The two Camp Wellfleet soldiers hit high fly balls that Kenny Rose caught in centerfield, and Bobby Snow fouled off two pitches before striking out with a mighty swing and miss.

Bound Brook players ran out to their positions. Jimmy was distracted watching Rachel taking practice grounders and throwing to first. You can spot a gifted athlete by the rhythm and grace of the movements. She had that smooth flow that advertised her skills. He watched as she glided to the ball, and in one fluid motion side-armed the ball to Bobby at first.

"Second base," yelled out Ben Sr. as he caught Benny's last warmup and threw a high ball that Hoopy had to jump to snag. "Guess I'm a little rusty," laughed the catcher.

"Batter up," barked out Jimmy as the Wellfleet hitter strode to the plate.

"Hi there, ump. How ya doing? Long time no see!" Ted Bowers tapped his bat on the plate, dug some dirt with his back foot and took his stance.

Jim froze. The voice, the cocky swagger pulled him back to Korea. He couldn't breathe, images flooded and he was there again. He checked his weapon, his eyes scanned the field, and his mind checked the positions of his men. Fielders were crouched, but no enemy was in sight. There was no snow, no mountains, just parked cars and people watching, but the Chinese could be hiding anywhere.

Smack, the pitch hit the catcher's mitt.

He flinched.

Silence.

"So Ump, you gonna make a call? Ball or strike?" The smug voice scraped down Jimmy's spine.

"Got to admit it was a bit outside," said Ben Sr.

"Ball," said Jimmy.

"Geez ump, you look like you seen a ghost. You all right?" Ted Bowers smirked at him, gave him a wink and then looked back at the pitcher.

Benny's pitch was right down the middle. Bowers lined it over second base for a clean single, but never stopped. He rounded first and steamed toward second as the surprised centerfielder hurried a throw to Rachel covering the bag. She caught the ball cleanly, but before she could swipe a tag, Bowers barreled into her. He never even tried to slide, but still standing up, he wrapped her in a bear hug, continued two more steps past the base and fell to the ground on top of a startled Rachel.

It was as if time froze. Without even thinking, Jimmy was on the move. Bowers rose to a kneeling position, still astride Rachel.

"Gee, I'm sorry. Here, let me clean you off." He brushed his hand across Rachel's chest. Then as he stood up, he pulled her to her feet. "Let me give you a kiss to apologize."

Jimmy flew into him with a football tackle. The two fell to the ground, with Jimmy unleashing a relentless flurry of blows with both hands. Ted shielded his face with his left forearm while countering with right-hand punches to Jimmy's side. Suddenly everybody was moving toward the combatants.

A circle surrounded the struggle, with the two bodies locked in a clinch, neither one now able to get any clean punches.

"Break it up!" yelled George. "Ben, Buddy, grab them."
Arms reached out and yanked the two fighters apart. Bowers
seemed content to let it end, but Jimmy struggled against the
restraint.

"It's been you, I should have seen it. You bastard, I'll
kill you. Stay away from my family or I'll break your skull. I
should have taken care of you in Korea."

"Calm down, Curtis. What's your problem, just a little
accident with the lady here. I apologize."

It took Ben, Hoopy and Buddy to drag Jimmy away, but
he kept fighting to get loose. "Bowers, you are a sick bastard.
You should have died in Korea. If I see you again, it will be
your last day on earth."

"I'd like to see you try, you gimp!" yelled Ted.

Dick Cochran, Eddie Maker and Kenny Rose blocked
Ted from going after Jimmy.

"Sergeant, I think you and your men need to return to
your base," said Cochran.

Bowers dusted himself off. "Ramsdell -- Dalby, meet
me at the Jeep. Curtis, you'll always be a loser, can't even keep
your woman."

Jimmy made one more lunge, but Hoopy blocked him.
Bowers spit on the ground, turned, walked off the field and
jumped into the army vehicle driven by Ramsdell. The stunned
group just stared at the cloud of dust as the vehicle bounced
over the ruts and took a left on the paved road.

Jim took a step toward Rachel. "Are you okay?"

"Leave me alone, will you? What do you think, I'm
some little girl who needs protecting? I can take care of myself.
I've been doing just fine while you were off playing soldier."
She grabbed her glove and cap and stomped back to her
position at second.

Jim hesitated, then turned, limped to the Packard and spun its wheels as he drove off too fast.

The teams finished the game in a listless daze. Wellfleet pulled a young Gene Howland from the spectators to fill Bowers' spot and Bound Brook plugged in Joey Pierce and Jerry Paine, who had just arrived. Spectators watched with muted interest; the confrontation had sucked the life from the traditionally passionate competition. There was a sense of just wanting to get it finished. If anyone cared, the final score was:

Wellfleet 10 – Bound Brook 8

*****

Peter Burke sat in his Willis Jeepster, with a floppy safari hat pulled down low. He couldn't take his eyes off Rachel. She was not only beautiful and intelligent, but also an athlete. When the army guy tackled her, he was halfway out of the Jeep before he restrained himself. The man with the limp got there way before he could have. Peter wasn't sure who the man was, but obviously he had some connection to Rachel.

It was probably just as well that he didn't come to the rescue of the damsel in distress. Peter had grown to five-foot-ten, and had a slim but well-built frame. He looked like an athlete, which was so far from the truth. He had never played sports and never won a fight in his life. Instead of saving Rachel, he probably would have made a fool of himself.

The handsome, confident college professor was a fraud. He marveled at where this new version of himself had materialized. Peter still saw himself as the awkward, skinny, shrimp of a boy, with ears and nose too big for his face and a mop of unruly hair. He was an only child who had disappointed his depressed mother and incurred the wrath of his successful but alcoholic father.

He had never been picked for sports and was bullied by the other boys. He had avoided other kids whenever possible. His world was between the pages of thrilling classics, where he could imagine himself slaying dragons and saving fair maidens. He idealized many of the girls he knew; in his mind they were fair ladies of noble birth. In reality, they treated him with contempt and displayed no graceful traits.

One event had seared his memory and now it flashed back to mind. Peter was twelve again, with a mad crush on Sally Rose. Sally and Pammy Costa stood on the fringe of the crowd at the Wednesday night square dance behind the Wellfleet Town Hall. He was good at square dancing, but he was always a fill-in male partner with a group of adults. Now he mustered his courage.

"Choose your partners," the caller barked out.

He started toward the two pretty girls and his eyes locked with Sally's. He froze as Sally's smiling face turned to revulsion. She swung her head and pigtails flew as she turned away. Then Pammy noticed Peter and her face smirked with contempt as a sneering laugh dripped from her pursed lips. With their backs turned, the two girls giggled their disdain for him.

He ran, pushing through the squares of dancers that started to form. Then he was on his bike, pedaling frantically in the twilight. Flying, fleeing, tears blinding his vision, he vowed never to risk being scorned again. After that, he built his secret hideout, his safe refuge, where rejection and derision did not exist. It was where the fair maidens of his dreams were demure and graceful.

Then in his late teens he had had a growth spurt, and somehow as an adult the pieces of his face and body had come together. Now other people found him handsome, and his intelligence shone through, but deep down he knew he was still a fraud.

His love of literature had led to a good college, excellent grades and the attention of the English Department faculty. A master's degree and then a Ph.D. had landed him his spot at Boston University. It was only as an instructor, but students loved his class. The department chair had called him into his office at the end of the spring semester and offered him the first summer session with a hint of a future assistant-professor position.

In front of a classroom, he was a different person. He was on stage playing a part, like one of the heroic characters he admired. He strutted and spoke in a strong, poised voice with a flair for the dramatic. At times, he shocked himself. It was as if another being took over his body. He did not understand it, but his love of literature had turned him into a passionate and charismatic teacher. When the class ended, he came plummeting back to earth, like Icarus having flown too close to the sun.

Several pretty girls had flirted with the charming college instructor, but Peter wasn't fooled. They might have been infatuated, but he knew their real motive was to curry favor and get a good grade. They saw him as a conquest and a means to an end. Those girls did not measure up to his ideal. They were shallow, with no intellect or talents other than their physical charms.

This was different, though. Now, the feeling that absorbed his body left him shaken. This girl, this . . . woman, was the epitome of all the heroines in his favorite books. Now she was in peril. The man who had tackled her exuded evil, Peter could feel it. However, she was clearly angry with the man with the limp who had tried to help her.

He remembered a Shakespeare quote from Coriolanus: "Action is eloquence," and his mind developed a scenario, a plot. Like Maid Marion, this women was in peril, but there was no Robin Hood to save her. She needed a champion. He could be the one; hadn't the young Arthur, a mere squire, pulled the sword from the stone and become a king? A king who protected the weak and fought for justice. Maybe this was the purpose of his adult transformation. If he could be strong and confident in the classroom, why not in his real life? It was time to stand up to the evil in the world. He had an idea.

Chapter 18
Rachel & Jim
Friday Night, July 4th

Rachel slammed the car door and kicked the tire. She stormed into Rob's cottage, grabbed a towel and headed for the outside shower. She tore off her clothes and let the cold water hit her face. The steady torrent of liquid washed away the dust and sweat. A deep breath and then the tears began to flow in choking sobs. The anger, pain and frustration seeped from her pores and streamed down her body. She grabbed the bar of Ivory soap and rubbed with all her strength.

Even with her body washed clean, she still felt dirty. The memory of the man's hands made her shudder. Who was that guy? Something about the man was foul: a malevolence that seeped from his being and made her shudder. What was Jimmy's connection? Obviously, they had a history and he hated the man.

Thoughts of Jimmy made the tears begin again. The look of forlorn rejection on his face when she had yelled at him was heartbreaking. Hadn't he been through enough? Why did she have to make it worse? Sure, he had his problems, but he was basically a decent man. He just looked so . . . lost. She didn't want to be back in his life, twelve years of wasted efforts were enough. But she still felt a responsibility.

The swirl of muddled thoughts and emotions was overwhelming. She turned off the shower and pulled the towel from the hook. She scoured her body with the rough fabric until her skin was red. She made a turban to cover her wet hair, stomped naked into the cabin and threw herself onto Rob's bed.

The light in the bedroom was dim when she opened her eyes, and silence filled the space as she came back to the real world. Rachel remembered the game and its repercussions. She longed for Rob to hold her and listen to her thoughts. He wasn't there, and with his holiday double-shift, he wouldn't be until late that night.

She rolled over and put her feet on the floor, reached for her small suitcase and pulled out a set of clean clothes. In the bathroom mirror, she studied her tangle of unruly hair. Never fall asleep with wet hair. The brush snagged and tugged as she tried to make her tresses fall into place. Oh well, she huffed and gave up.

She slipped her feet into a pair of sandals, grabbed her car keys and headed out the door. It was time to talk with Jimmy, get some issues settled and find out who that wicked man was. She had a nagging feeling that Jimmy needed help.

On the ride to the Curtis house, she tried to focus and take things one at a time. It was 7:30 with the sun low and the air heavy with humidity. She let the breeze from the open window blow in her face. Driving past houses, she saw extra cars in the driveways and caught a whiff of grilled barbeque in the air. Families were sharing the spirit of the nation's birth on this festive day.

There were no cars in the Curtis driveway. The lingering scent of charred wood hung in the dank air. The house had an empty forlorn look that matched Rachel's mood. Mabel was with her parents, but she wondered where Jimmy had gone. She felt a knot in her throat and pushed away the feeling. Whatever was going on with Jimmy would have to wait and the talk would be some other day.

*****

Jim Curtis sat at the bar of the Old Colony Tap in Provincetown. The bar was just starting to fill and the owner,

Frank Days, nodded a welcome to the regulars, largely fishermen. It was the holiday, but some occupations didn't take days off. He saw a few familiar faces, but these were serious drinkers and for the most part, they kept to themselves.

"Jim? Jimmy Curtis?" A man about his age leaned on the bar and gave him a grin. "I thought that was you. Hey man, good to see you. Haven't seen much of you since I was trying to guard you in high school. Wow, what a team you guys had."

"Is that Mike Tasha? How are you? What are you doing these days?"

"Took over my Dad's plumbing business. Can't complain. Business is so good I can hardly keep up with it, and I guess it beats the hard life of fishing."

The two old sports rivals fell into an easy banter, catching up on mutual acquaintances. Jim told Mike he was working at the Camp Wellfleet PX for the summer, and what Rob and Hoopy were doing. In no time at all there were a half dozen empty bottles in front of him and almost that many in front of Tasha. Jim could feel the buzz and his tongue was thick when he spoke.

"Say Mike, you know you must be the only person I know who hasn't asked me about Korea. Gotta tell you that I really appreciate it."

"Yah well, I was in the Pacific fighting the Japanese in the big one. We were moving from one island after another, trying to drive the Japs out of their caves. I know I don't want to talk about it and I'd guess you don't either. Civilians don't get it. They think it's all like John Wayne. Unless they've been there, they wouldn't understand. And well, the two of us have been there; John Wayne was only there in the movies."

Jim nodded.

Mike squinted in the smoky haze of the bar. "I got a question for you, though. You know any army guys from Camp Wellfleet?"

"Why do you ask?"

Mike shook a Marlboro out of its pack. "See these? Brian Francis has been going around town, selling stuff real cheap, mainly cigarettes. He claims he found some crates that washed up on shore. But some people are saying he got it from an army guy, and it ain't legit."

"Hmm . . . Yes, I do know a guy that would do that."

"Look, I'm not trying to get anyone in trouble. So you didn't hear nothing from me. Never should have brought it up, but you know, sometimes you just get curious."

An image came back to Jim. He was in Korea and Sergeant Wright was telling him about what he saw Bowers do to a Korean woman.

"You okay, man? You've got that look, you know, that thousand-yard stare. I've been there . . . Sorry, I should know better than to bring up things like that. Must be the beers."

"I'm okay. It's just that today I saw a man I never thought I would see again, never wanted to see again. He was in Korea with me, and I think he might be the army guy you're talking about. Last time I heard about him, a friend of mine, Sergeant David Wright, was telling me some really bad stuff the guy had done to a local girl. Wright told me he was going to report him."

"Damn, sounds like a nasty type, so what happened? Did he get reported?"

"The next day, Sergeant Wright was killed. It got chalked up to a Chinese recon patrol, but I always wondered. Anyway, turns out the girl's father was some village official and he filed a complaint. I got asked if I knew anything. We were in different platoons, but the same company. Well, I shoulda kept my mouth shut, but I told them what Wright had told me. Of course, by then Wright was dead and it was just hearsay. I guess the guy was disciplined and shipped back to the states."

"Sounds like good-riddance to me."

"Yeah, except I saw him again today, and I got a feeling he knows I reported him."

Chapter 19
Elaine – Murder Most Foul

"Nothing in his life
Became him like the leaving it"
William Shakespeare – Macbeth: Act 1, Scene 4

Saturday, July 5th

Elaine Samuels finished getting dressed for her waitressing shift at the Mayflower Café in Provincetown. She tucked the black t-shirt into her snug white shorts. Her black and white outfit fit the restaurant's official dress code, but the way it fit her voluptuous figure was borderline appropriate for a family establishment. Hey, it wasn't her fault God gave her this figure.

She brushed her luxurious, raven hair, pulled it tight into a ponytail and tied a white ribbon in a bow. She squinted into the faded and cracked mirror. Her striking features never needed makeup; her olive complexion was clear, but there was a hint of wrinkles at the corner of her eyes. One more glance and then she got up and went out the front door of her ramshackle cottage in one of the deep hollows of Bound Brook. The cottage was all she had left from her parents. It was a wonder they had left her anything at all. Neither one had made it to see fifty. That's what boozing every day will do to you.

Beep Beep. The horn of Ivy Smith's old Ford Sedan sounded as she pulled into the driveway. Ivy lived in Wellfleet and worked at one of the other restaurants in Provincetown. Fortunately, for Elaine, she had a car.

"Thanks for the lift, Ivy."

"No problem, just remember I'm getting out earlier than you tonight."

"That's okay. Moose Parker will give me a ride home."

Elaine hoped it would be a good night, and that the tips would make it worth plastering a phony smile on her face and hustling hot plates to obnoxious tourists.

*****

Rob Caldwell pulled into the Police and Fire Department building and parked beside Chief Foster's Bound Brook police cruiser. He took the steps two at a time to the tiny headquarters on the top of the building over the Fire Department's two engines.

Diane Ellis, the dispatcher, looked up. "Hi Rob. You clocking out for the night?"

"I sure am. Hey, the Chief got a minute for me?"

"I heard that, sure, come on in," boomed a voice from Foster's office.

"So, how's the weekend been going, Chief?"

"The usual stupidity. Drunks getting burned with fireworks they shouldn't be handling, drunks having bonfires on the beaches without permits, drunks getting into arguments at Art's, Drunks . . . well you get the theme."

Rob laughed. "Yup, I think I handled a lot of those calls myself. Say, you still only need me for the day shift tomorrow?"

"That should do it. Skip and I have just about finished breaking in the two new full-time summer guys. I know you want the summer off, but I hope I can call on you if we get in a pinch."

"You know you can count on me." He touched the brim of his cap to the Chief and waved to Diane on his way out.

"You got any Saturday night plans?" asked Diane.

"In fact I've got a hot date," he laughed.

"Well, have fun, you earned it."

He exhaled, glad to be finished dealing with brash holiday partiers for the night. He hoped he could be more help to Rachel.

When he had gotten off his late shift the night before he had found her waiting for him. Her face was blotchy and her eyes were red. He listened while she poured out her feelings. The part about the army guy at the game was particularly disturbing.

"So you said Jim knew this guy?"

"Not just knew him, he definitely hated him. He told him he wished he had killed him in Korea. I went over to the house last night to talk to him, and maybe find out more. Well, Jimmy wasn't there. I'm afraid I know where he went -- well, maybe not the exact bar, but a bar somewhere."

"I'll talk to the Chief and maybe Chief Fleming in Wellfleet. Might file a complaint at Camp Wellfleet. I think that guy needs to be checked into."

"No, please don't. I just want it over. It's Jimmy I'm worried about."

"Me too, but not much we can do about it tonight. I think you need to get your mind off it. I'm not supposed to work tomorrow night. It'll be Saturday night. Let's splurge and get something to eat in Orleans at the Southward Inn. If we go early, maybe we can catch the second half of the double feature at the Cinema. We need to go on a real date."

When he got to his cottage, Rachel was already dressed and ready to go. "Hey, handsome, get changed and let's go. I'm planning on spending lots of your money."

*****

Salvatore "Sal" Santos scrubbed his calloused hands and used the tip of his jackknife to clean his nails. No matter how hard he scrubbed, he knew the smell of fish and diesel oil would still be there. Years on the water had darkened his complexion to a nutty brown, his face a leathery mask. He yanked a towel off the hook on the back of the bathroom door. He rubbed the moisture from his face and hands and threw the towel against the door. Sal was seething, and he needed to take it out on something or someone.

His only daughter, his youngest child, the baby of the family, Elizabeth, had been hurt. A vile man, a devil who did not know how to treat a woman, had wounded his sweetheart. His wife said he should go to the police, but Sal did not believe in the police. In his experience, in the old country, the police served justice to the rich people.

Police were not for people like Sal or Liz. They protected soldiers and government officials. The man was in the army, and nobody would do anything to him. He thought about going to the priest, but he didn't want to have to say aloud what had happened. Besides, he didn't want to turn the other cheek. If Sal wanted justice, he would get it himself.

He clenched his muscles; a life of pulling nets, cleaning fish and hefting baskets had hardened his lithe physique to chiseled stone. Sal pulled on a white undershirt his wife Maria had scrubbed clean. His anger would be quenched. Tonight he wasn't going fishing, tonight he was going hunting.

*****

Jim Curtis sat on the Provincetown pier and watched boats docking and unloading their catch of fish. The sun was setting over the bay and the scene looked like a postcard. He took the last drag of a Viceroy cigarette and flicked the butt it into the water. Smoking and drinking again, back to his old habits. He had kicked both in Korea, but he wasn't in the army anymore and the routines of living on the Cape were coming back—for good or bad.

A man walked past him headed to the end of the wharf. Jim's sixth sense tingled. The man was trying to be casual, but he was an amateur. He seemed to have one eye on Jimmy. The man's features were obscured; an oversized safari hat was pulled low over his face. Then the figure was just an outline in the glare of the setting sun. The man stopped at the edge of the pier, then turned and walked away.

"Hey, you, do I know you?"

The man increased his pace and kept walking. Strange . . . back in the army, he would have pursued, challenged and questioned the man. His behavior was definitely suspicious. No, Jim stayed where he was. He wasn't in the army. He reached for another cigarette and headed toward the Old Colony Tap. Maybe his answers were in a bottle of beer. He had never found them there before, but there was always a first time.

Later that night he climbed into the Packard. Instead of heading directly south toward Bound Brook, he drove down Commercial Street toward the West End and continued out to the rock jetty at the tip of P'town. He pulled over and admired the view on a perfect moonlit night. Then he took the back roads, before connecting to the new highway. Because of his route, he never saw Officer Tony Oliver sitting in the P'town cruiser waiting for drunks. Of course, Tony never saw him either.

*****

Simon Eldredge sat in his car outside the PX as the sun set low on the horizon. Something had been nagging at him ever since Thursday when he had reported the thefts to the Lieutenant. On his way back to the PX he had paused and watched that Sergeant walk away. Something about his silhouette—his shape, bearing and stride—struck a chord. It looked so much like the figure he had seen in the dim light the night before.

So he had returned to the base every night since, and watched and waited. His new confidence and determination now fired a need to catch the thief. *Nobody steals from an Eldredge,* his father's words pounded in his head.

A figure in civilian clothes emerged from the barracks, walked to a Jeep, got in, and drove toward the gate. Simon put in the clutch and started his engine. He slowed and waved to the familiar guard on his way out to the highway. Simon kept his quarry in sight as they headed north toward Bound Brook, Truro and Provincetown.

Thursday night, Friday night and now Saturday night, Bowers' routine was the same. He drove to Provincetown and paid visits to several of the bars and restaurants. Simon sat on a bench on the corner of the main street and the entrance to the town pier that had a huge parking lot. Bowers seemed to spend the most time at the Mayflower.

Simon felt a calmness and contentment that was entirely new. Sitting and watching the ebb and flow of people having fun and enjoying the evening, he felt for the first time that he was gaining control of his life. Now he had a chance to succeed at something and prove his father and family wrong. Unfortunately, this Sergeant Bowers wanted to destroy all that.

Part Two – Revenge

"Revenge this foul and unnatural murder."
William Shakespeare – Hamlet: Act 1, Scene 5

"These violent delights have violent ends."
William Shakespeare - Romeo and Juliet: Act 2, Scene 6

"And if you wrong us shall we not revenge?"
William Shakespeare - Merchant of Venice: Act 3, Scene 1

"Revenge should have no bounds."
William Shakespeare – Hamlet: Act 4, Scene 7

"Vengeance is in my heart, death in my hand,
Blood and revenge are hammering in my head."
William Shakespeare - Titus Andronicus: Act 2, Scene 3

Chapter 20

"O villain, villain, smiling damned villain."
William Shakespeare – Hamlet: Act 1, Scene 5

Sunday Morning, July 6th

The incessant ringing hurt Rob's ears. He rolled out of bed trying not to wake Rachel, and stumbled to the phone. *Damn thing was the worst mistake I ever made!*

"Hello, who is this and what time is it?"

"Good morning to you, Mary Sunshine. It's your friendly police dispatcher. The time at the sound of my voice is 6:25 a.m. Your presence is requested by your neighborhood Chief of Police."

"Very funny, Diane, but last night was my final shift. I'm off for the summer."

"Yes, Rob, I am aware of that. However, sometimes murders have a way of changing schedules."

"What . . . Why didn't you say that? Who was murdered?"

"Well, that's what you can help figure out. The Chief needs you to join him at Bound Brook Pond as quick as you can get there."

The line went dead with a click. Rob was awake now, even without coffee; a murder tends to perk up your senses. He tiptoed into the bedroom and grabbed his uniform from the back of the chair.

"Did I hear you say murder?"

"Ah, yes. I don't know any details, just that it's out at Bound Brook Pond. I have to hurry; the Chief wants me there right away."

He finished buttoning his uniform shirt, grabbed his tie and hat, leaned over and gave Rachel a kiss on the cheek. "Last night was a lot of fun. We need to do more of that. Both the date and the other stuff, you know. See you tonight, I hope."

Ten minutes later, he parked at Bound Brook Pond. The police cruiser was there and Rob recognized Doc Carter's car and two other cars that looked familiar. What wasn't familiar was an army Jeep. Still fiddling with his loose tie, he walked down the embankment. Chief Foster was there with Skip Parker, Doc Carter, Henry Newcomb and Russell Ormsby. Newcomb was Chairman of the Board of Selectmen and Ormsby was the Town Clerk and Treasurer, as well as holding several other lesser titles. The pale body of a man wearing white skivvies was on the beach. The ashen face and blue lips told him all he needed to know.

"Hi, Rob, welcome to the party," said Skip. "This is becoming too much of a habit. Two murders in less than six months must be some sort of Brook Bound record."

Chief Foster gave Skip one of his looks. "No time for chit chat. I want to get a start on this before the State Troopers arrive. I asked Henry and Russell to stay; they are witnesses, top town officials and also deputized Town Constables. So, bottom line is, Doc doesn't think this was an accidental drowning."

Doc Carter winked at Rob. "Yes, based on my medical degree, years of experience, oh, and also judging by the broken clavicle and the deep depression in his skull . . . Yup, I'd say he didn't accidentally drown. Also, there's an ugly bite mark on his hand that looks human."

Foster shook his head. "Bunch of jokers we got here. Listen, the Troopers and D.A.'s Office will take over the investigation like they do with all murders. However, we'll probably be needed to do some of the early grunt work and fact gathering. I want to get started right away."

"So what do we know?" asked Rob.

The Chief looked at Skip. "Bring him up to speed, will you? I need to radio the station."

"Henry and Russell got here about 5:35 to do some early fishing."

"The early bird gets the worm, but the early worm gets the fish," chuckled Henry.

"Yup," said Russell, "this was definitely the biggest fish I ever caught."

Skip rolled his eyes. "They spotted the body right away and woke up a neighbor to use their phone. There are too many tire tracks in the lot and too many footprints on the embankment to be of any use. The pond has been busy with the heat wave and the holiday weekend. The Chief has calls into Camp Wellfleet for anyone missing, and to all the surrounding PDs for anyone who saw the army Jeep last night. That's basically it."

They turned to the sound of the hulking Police Chief coming down the embankment. "Well, we've got some answers already," said Foster. "Diane told me that Camp Wellfleet reported that Sergeant Ted Bowers never returned to the base last night, after leaving in an army Jeep. Also, the Provincetown Police said that Officer Oliver saw an army Jeep leaving P'town, heading south around closing time for the bars.

"There was a man driving with a woman passenger. Tony Oliver recognized Elaine Samuels as the passenger. Between the full moon and the bright streetlights, he was positive it was her. Provincetown's Chief is going to get Tony to give a full account of any other cars he remembers seeing around that time. One car he did see was Moose Parker's truck. Seems he drove past soon after the Jeep did."

Rob looked at the Chief. "Do you need one of us to go talk to Elaine?"

Foster nodded. "Yes, I will coordinate with everyone: State Police, P'town Police and Camp Wellfleet. Meanwhile, I need both Rob and Skip to go to Elaine's house. Determine if she is home. If she isn't home, we need to search this area for her. I'd hate to think we've got another victim out here. If she is home, let Diane know right away, then you need to bring her to the station to give us a full statement. Remember, she could be a murder suspect or at least a material witness.

"The State Police will meet you there. They may want to conduct the interrogation, so do not push the questions too far. If she is home though, I'd like to know how she got there, given that the Jeep is still here. After you get Elaine settled, I need you to go talk with Moose. Maybe he saw something."

Doc Carter spoke up. "I have an ambulance on its way to transport the body for the post mortem. I'll get you the results as soon as we know anything."

"Wellfleet PD are handling questions at Camp Wellfleet," added Foster. "I need to tell you all to keep your mouths closed about this murder. It could be anyone. I'm assuming, at least for now, that it wasn't any of us, but beyond that, everyone is a suspect."

"Oh, and Henry and Russell, I need this road and beach closed. Call one of the town specials and the highway crew. We'll need to do a full sweep of the surrounding area, especially any paths or trails. Hope we don't find another victim."

*****

Moose Parker pulled the covers over his head to block the hint of daylight that peeked through the curtains. It didn't feel right, something was off. Then he remembered he was at Elaine's house, sleeping in her parents' double bed. Elaine had some serious issues with her deceased parents and told Moose that she never went into their old room.

Sunday was a day off from his job with the Bound Brook Highway Department. Normally he would sleep late, but even though it was early, he was wide awake. He got out of bed and found his clothes tossed over the bedpost. He tiptoed into the kitchen and spotted a coffee pot. He could really use some, but he didn't want to wake up Elaine.

There was orange juice in the refrigerator and some glasses on the shelves. With a glass of juice in hand, he sat at the kitchen table and thought about the events of the previous night.

The confrontation with Ted at the pond was a dim memory. Working as a doorman and occasional bouncer, a brief physical encounter, even a violent one, was nothing new to Moose. Just another drunk who went too far. What he went over in his mind was what had happened when he had gotten to Elaine's house.

"Moose, you can sleep in my parents' room if you want. I mean, well, it would be fine if you slept in my bed with me. Not like anything has to happen, you know. Well . . . you're a nice guy, and I really owe you for saving me tonight."

"Wow, gee, Elaine, I think your parents' room would be fine. I'm sure you're safe now and I'll be in the next room."

"This is awkward, Moose, but I wondered if there was any chance that you like me. You know, more than just as a friend."

"Sure, I like you a lot. You are really pretty, and I always knew under that tough girl act was a sweetheart."

Elaine moved closer, reached up and touched his shoulder. Her fingers moved to the back of his neck and she pulled his head lower. Moose closed his eyes and felt the soft touch of her lips on his cheek.

"I was thinking we could be more than just friends," she whispered.

Moose pulled back. "Elaine, I don't know what to say. It's just well . . . I don't really like girls that way. I mean if I did, well, you would be the one, but . . . Damn, I already said too much!" He turned his head and pulled away.

"Oh. . . . Oh, I see . . ."

"Do you? You won't say anything, will you? I can't . . . well, do you understand? Nobody else can know."

"No, Moose, it's okay. Listen, you are a great guy and I would be honored to be your best friend. You know, I probably need a friend more than a lover. Maybe that's been my problem all along. Come here and give me a hug."

Moose had wrapped Elaine in a bear hug. Warm and comforting, it had felt good.

A sharp knock on the screen door snapped him back to reality. "Hello, anyone home? It's the Bound Brook Police."

Moose stepped through the living room to the front door. "What are the police doing here?"

"Moose, is that you? It's your brother, Skip; I thought that truck was yours."

"Hi, Moose, it's Rob Caldwell. We need to ask Elaine some questions. Is she here?"

"I'm here," called Elaine from the back bedroom. "Give me a minute. Sit down, I'll be right there."

The men pulled up kitchen chairs and sat down at the table. An awkward silence filled the air.

Elaine came out of the bedroom, wrapped in an oversized terry cloth robe. She walked over to Moose and gave him a kiss on the cheek.

"Good morning, sweetheart!"

Moose flushed. "Ah, yes. . . Good morning to you too."

Elaine sat in the remaining chair. "Rob, Skip, to what do I owe the honor of your visit at this hour of the morning?"

Skip looked at Rob. "Well, Elaine," said Rob, "were you in an army Jeep last night in Provincetown?"

"Yes, why? What does that matter?"

"Would you tell us where you went and who you were with?"

"Okay, sure, I was with an army guy I met at the Mayflower where I waitress. We drove out to Bound Brook Pond."

"And what happened there?"

"Well, if you must know the jerk tried to . . . well, you know . . . He tried to take advantage of me. He probably would have if Moose hadn't come along."

Rob glanced at Skip, then continued, "So, Moose, what did you do?"

"You know I work at the Mayflower with Elaine. So, when I saw her leave with that guy, I got a bad feeling. I think he's the same army guy that had the fight with Jimmy at the baseball game. You know who I mean; everyone's been talking about it."

"So what did you do?"

"Well, I asked Frankie, the bartender, to lock up for me and I took off to Bound Brook Pond. Just had a hunch."

Moose paused and looked at Rob and his brother. "What's the problem, and what does this have to do with the police?"

"Just keep going, you are doing fine," said Rob.

"Well, when I got there, I heard Elaine screaming at the guy. It was obvious he was hurting her. So I jumped out of my truck and ran down to the pond. Elaine was running away from him and I told her to get in the truck."

Elaine broke in, "The guy was trying . . . you know. Anyway, I told him to stop and when he wouldn't I bit his hand. That was the only way I could get away from him. What, is he filing charges or something? He's the one that should get arrested."

Rob turned back to Moose. "So what did you do? Anything happen between the army guy and you?"

"Well, yes, he was whining about how his hand hurt, like he was some victim. So I came right at him; nailed him with two hands to the solar plexus, got him good with the heels of my hands, knocked the wind out of him. Then I told him he better stay away from Elaine, and I'd better not see him at the Mayflower again."

"Moose came right back to the truck. Must have only been about two minutes. Then he drove me home. I was pretty upset, but thank God he was there." She leaned toward him and patted his arm.

"Moose,'" Rob broke in, "did you have anything with you? Was it just your hands that hit him?"

"Yes, I've been handling drunks and breaking up fights for years. You learn a few tricks when you're a bouncer. You know, nothing takes the fight out of someone more than having the wind knocked out of them." He looked at Elaine. "Listen, I don't know if this guy filed charges, but he got less than he deserved. What are two police doing here? It's not like I killed the guy or anything."

Skip looked at Rob. Moose grabbed Elaine's arm. "What, what does that look mean? He isn't . . . No way, I just pushed him. . . This isn't happening . . . Tell us what's going on."

Rob stood up. "I need the two of you to get dressed and come down to the station with us. I can't tell you anything more, but it is serious and we need you to make statements."

"Elaine, I've got to use your phone to call the station," said Skip.

Chapter 21
Trooper Stewart

"Then murder's out of tune,
And sweet revenge grows harsh"
William Shakespeare – Othello: Act 5, Scene 2

Sunday Afternoon, July 6th

State Trooper Don Stewart sat in the cramped office of Police Chief Bill Foster. With him was a new Trooper, Michael O'Connor, who had just completed his probationary stage.

"So we took the statements from Arnold Parker and Elaine Samuels, although I guess her legal name is Stevens." Trooper Stewart looked at his notepad. "They both give the same story. Parker's truck was searched, and no signs of a murder weapon or club of any kind. We don't have the autopsy report, but those wounds were not made by hand."

"Yes, but he could have ditched the weapon. I know I would have," blurted Trooper O'Connor. Both Stewart and Foster gave him looks. "Sorry, I'll keep quiet."

Stewart continued, "Well, they both give identical stories. I couldn't trip them up. If Parker killed Sergeant Bowers, the DA probably wouldn't go for First Degree. Not my call, but the woman would claim he was defending her from a rape."

Foster nodded. "Look, we need to go by the evidence, but let me tell what I know about Moose. He's not the smartest guy on the block, which means he couldn't make up a good story. Now Elaine is savvy, she could concoct a good one, but Moose isn't quick enough to stay with the storyline. We could charge him with simple assault, he admitted that, but the real crime here is a murder. I think we need to keep looking. Something tells me there is a more complicated story here."

"Oh, I agree," said Stewart. "I just got more information and I need to bring you up to speed. By the way, I talked to the DA and he has agreed that because you and Bill Fleming in Wellfleet are retired State Troopers, you can be part of the active investigation. But only you two. If you need Rob or Skip to do simple errands that's fine, but no questioning or investigating. That is reserved for you and Fleming, and most of it should be done in my presence if at all possible."

"Yes, we don't need the locals messing this up," said O'Connor.

Stewart glared at the rookie. "Trooper O'Connor, please wait for us outside."

"But I need to hear what you're saying, I . . ."

"Trooper, outside, now!"

O'Connor grabbed his hat and with one backward glance went out of the office.

Stewart lowered his voice. "Chief, I'm sorry but I've got a problem here. This kid's father is high up in the Department; you know who he is, I think."

Foster nodded. "Oh yes, I know his father. We go way-way-back, and let me just say we are not each other's fans. Honestly, he is the major reason why I retired early. Long story."

"Well, the kid is on some sort of fast track, and now I'm supposed to be grooming him to be my replacement. I just got promoted to corporal, and I need to move to a district that has a corporal slot, but not until this case is solved."

"Congratulations, but I'm sorry we'll be losing you here on the Cape."

Stewart leaned closer. "Just between us, I'm worried about this kid. It's not the political pull; hey if he was good it wouldn't matter. I think you saw the problem; he's impulsive, and doesn't take direction well. I heard he would have washed out already if it wasn't for the old man."

"Oh, that sounds great."

Stewart shook his head. "Yup, and it gets worse. With my new rank and murder-cases knowledge, the DA has given me the lead on this case, but I've got to include "Junior" in on everything, so he can get the experience. I just want to clue you in. I'll try to keep a rein on him, but, well . . . you know politics. The kid could be a loose cannon."

There was a knock on the office door and Diane Ellis stuck her head in. "Chief, call for Trooper Stewart from the DA's Office. Just pick up in here and I'll hang up."

Foster picked up the phone and handed it to the State Trooper.

"Hello, yes . . . alright . . ." Stewart nodded while the voice on the phone spoke. "Yes, I've got it. I'll fill in Chief Foster."

Trooper Stewart handed the receiver to Foster, who hung it up. "As you know the DA is coordinating all the information now. I am his representative on the ground. Everything is funneled through me and then passed on to him."

"Got it," said the Chief.

"I guess I need to get the rookie back in here." Stewart got up and opened the door. "O'Connor come in . . . But I need you to just listen, got it?"

"Yes, Corporal Stewart."

"Let me summarize what we know so far. Camp Wellfleet has Army CIS investigators arriving sometime today. In the meantime, Chief Fleming in Wellfleet has learned a lot about our victim, Sergeant Theodore "Ted" Bowers. Bowers is, or was, a highly decorated nine-year veteran of World War Two and the Korean Conflict. Although his war record is outstanding, Chief Fleming knows enough to read between the lines. There is a reason he was sitting on the sand dunes of Cape Cod. Sergeant Bowers doesn't seem to have been a model soldier when back in the USA.

"But let me move on. Fleming interviewed a Simon Eldredge, Manager of the PX, and George Gilmore, his assistant. Of course we know George, he's the Bound Brook School principal. They both said the PX had items stolen from their inventory, before the store had even opened. Simon Eldredge believes the thief is Sergeant Bowers. Can't prove anything yet, but we'll know more when CIS checks his army background.

"Provincetown PD talked to the Mayflower Café, where Elaine met Bowers and where Parker was working that night. The bartender, a Frankie Reis, confirms that Bowers met Elaine and they left together to go to Bound Brook Pond. He says that both he and Parker had a feeling about Bowers, and thought that Elaine might be in trouble. So Parker left for the Pond and Reis said that's all he knows."

"I think I know our murderer," blurted O'Connor.

"Trooper, what did I say?"

"Sorry, Corporal, it's just I know who threatened him."

"Son, if you are talking about Jimmy Curtis," said Foster, "the whole town knows that."

"So why haven't you arrested him then?"

"Trooper, for the last time, I need you to be quiet!" barked Stewart.

Foster rolled his eyes. "Thank you, Trooper Stewart. Like I was saying, everyone in town has heard about the fight at the baseball game between Bowers and Curtis. If that was all it took to prove a murder, well, I wish it was so simple."

Stewart glared at O'Connor. "Officers Caldwell and Parker are looking for Curtis to bring him in for questioning. I gather that Curtis and Bowers had a nasty history together that went back to Korea."

*****

Jim Curtis stared out at the blue rippled surface of Bound Brook Bay. He seemed to be spending a lot of time lately, just sitting and staring at the waters of Cape Cod. Its gentle motion and soothing sound was a hypnotic balm. Too many thoughts ran through his mind. His fight with Bowers had triggered a jumble of images from his past. Too many confusing unresolved issues: Bowers, Rachel, Rob, even memories and regrets about his father's premature death. It was probably why he had gone back to the bottle. He needed the numbing elixir to dull the pain and confusion. So, he sat at the end of the pier, sneaking sips from a half-empty bottle.

"Hi, Jimmy." He looked up at the face of Bing Tyler, the Bound Brook Harbormaster.

"Hello, Bing."

"Say Jimmy, I don't know how to tell you this, but the police are looking for you."

"Why the hell are they looking for me? Is sitting on the pier and getting drunk a crime?"

"No, if it was, the jails would be full. You mean you haven't heard about the murder of that army guy?"

"Geez, no. What murder, what army guy, what are you talking about?"

"Jim, I just know the police wanted to talk to you about an army guy you knew in Korea. The same one you had the fight with at the baseball game."

Jimmy felt like he'd been slapped. "Bowers? You mean he's dead? Well, jeez, guess it couldn't happen to a nicer guy. Who says life ain't fair?"

"Look Jim, let me give you a lift down to the station. You're in no shape to drive."

Jimmy staggered to his feet. "Take a drive with you? Sure, Bing, that would be nice. You can tell me all about what's been going on and what I missed the past couple of years."

*****

State Trooper O'Connor sat on the top step of the Bound Brook PD and stared down the long stairway. Stewart had kicked him out of the meeting; well, his excuse was that O'Connor should wait for the amateur cops to bring in Curtis. He knew the real reason: they didn't want to share. They wanted all the glory of arresting the murderer and solving the crime. Wait until he told his father about the shabby way he had been treated.

An old pickup truck with the words *Bound Brook Harbormaster* painted on its side pulled into the small parking lot. A man stumbled out of the passenger door before the truck stopped rolling.

"Jimmy Curtis, wait for me," yelled the driver.

O'Connor bounded down the stairs. "Are you Curtis?" he snarled.

Jimmy snapped to attention and waved a sloppy salute. "Sure am, Sergeant First Class James Curtis. Who the hell are you?"

"Turn around, hands behind your back. You are under arrest…"

Jimmy shoved O'Connor, then staggered back against the truck.

"You're resisting arrest. Down on the ground, now!"

Jimmy connected with a sloppy right-hand jab and the trooper's uniform hat went flying.

O'Connor grabbed Jim, spun him around and slammed him against the truck. He yanked his arm behind him and snapped handcuffs on Jim's right wrist. But Jim whirled around and planted a kick in O'Connor's groin. The trooper toppled to the ground, grabbing his crotch.

"What the hell is going on out here?" yelled Foster from the top of the stairs.

Bing Tyler stepped in front of Curtis, "Geez, Jimmy, calm down."

Trooper Stewart flew down the stairs, three at a time. "Goddamn O'Connor, can't I leave you alone for five minutes?"

"The S.O.B. attacked me. You'd better arrest him for assaulting an officer and resisting arrest. He's lucky you got here, or else . . ."

"O'Connor, shut up! What a fiasco!"

Chapter 22

"Just the facts, ma'am"
Jack Webb as Joe Friday - Dragnet 1951

Sunday , Late Afternoon, July 6th

Rob sat down on the edge of the bed and pulled off his
shiny black shoes. He paused, took a deep breath, stood up,
shucked off his uniform and threw it in the corner of the room.
He wouldn't need it again for the rest of the summer. Stripping
off the rest of his clothes, he grabbed a towel hanging on the
bedpost and wrapped it around his waist.

"So, are you going to tell me what's going on?" Rachel
called from the kitchen. "There's all kinds of rumors that I
heard when I was in the pharmacy. Did they really arrest
Jimmy?"

"Let me rinse off in the shower first, and then I'll tell
you the whole story." He went outside, to the only shower the
cottage had until the renovations were finished. The cold water
lowered his temperature and his mood. What a frustrating day!
He knew Rachel was dying to hear what had happened to Jim,
so he made it quick.

Wrapped in his towel he sat down on a kitchen chair,
his wet legs dripping on the wooden floor. Rachel stood near
the sink, her arms wrapped tightly across her chest.

"Yes, Jimmy is being held in the Provincetown jail.
Right now it's just a drunk and disorderly charge. There's a
jerk, a rookie State Trooper, wants to charge him with assault
on an officer and resisting arrest, but Don Stewart says he can
get that dropped, at least he thinks he can. It's complicated.
When he sobers up, he'll be held for questioning about the

murder of Sergeant Theodore Bowers. Bowers is the jerk that grabbed you at the game."

"That's ridiculous! Jimmy wouldn't do that. I know he hated the man, I mean who wouldn't, but murder? No, no, not Jimmy."

"Well, the murder investigation is just starting. Listen, I'm off the police force, at least for the summer. I told Foster not to call me back to work. I need to clear Jim and find the murderer, and I can't do that if I'm stuck following official orders."

"So it's that serious. I mean, they really think he did it?"

"Jimmy threatened to kill the man, in front of about a hundred witnesses, including you. On top of that, the Provincetown Police questioned the bars in town, and Jimmy was at the Old Colony Tap until closing time. Bowers was at the Mayflower, practically across the street, until closing. He could have followed him. So, motive, means and opportunity; they got two out of three, actually probably all three."

"So what can we do? We can't let Jimmy get convicted for something we know he didn't do."

"I already contacted Attorney Snow in Provincetown. He'll represent Jim until he can arrange another lawyer with homicide experience if they press murder charges. I talked to Mabel and told her not to worry about the expense. I've got it covered."

"So you really think they are going to charge him? He is innocent; you and I know he couldn't murder anyone. They can't do that."

"Do we know he's innocent? Of course you and I don't believe he did it, but he's a soldier, he's killed people, he's trained, he is certainly capable of it."

Rachel slammed her fist on the counter. "Well, I'm not going to just stand around while he gets railroaded for something he didn't do. What can I do to help?"

"Moose and Elaine Samuels were probably the last people to see Bowers alive. That is, if you believe that they didn't kill him, and honestly, I don't think they did. The police haven't ruled them out completely, but they are looking harder at Jim."

Rob stood up. "I need to change, then I'm going to the Mayflower and talk with Moose and the bartender. Then I'm going to the Colony Tap and find out who saw Jimmy, and find out anything else I can."

"What about me?"

"I heard that Elaine has the night off, so you can go talk with her. Bring a note pad. Ask her any details she can remember. Did she see anyone else out there? Did they pass any cars? Ask her what she and Bowers talked about before he got rough with her. Ask her to tell you in detail what she did, what Bowers did, and what Moose did. She will say that she already told the police, but she and Moose went to school with Jimmy and us; I can't believe she wants to see him convicted. Convince her how important it is."

*****

Peter Burke, Ph.D., unloaded a stack of 2x4s. He swatted a mosquito on the back of his neck and wiped sweat from his forehead. He was on the edge of an eerie environment, an ancient geological depression in the sand dunes of South Wellfleet that looked more like the bayous of Louisiana. To get there he had driven one of the many cart paths abandoned years earlier, when horses gave way to automobiles. His Willys

Jeepster with 4-wheel drive was necessary to navigate the rutted, overgrown trail.

At times the brush and tiny new growth of scrub pine made the primitive road almost invisible. However, Peter knew the route like the back of his hand. He had been coming here since he was a child when his grandfather had showed it to him. On his first visit, it had immediately triggered his imagination and matched the fantasies of his fairy tale readings.

Years later he had learned about its geological and biological significance. Peter's first roommate in college had been in the forestry department, with a fervent interest in trees, shrubs and all types of flora. One spring break, while the wealthy students went to exotic places, Peter had brought Joseph to cold, windswept Cape Cod. When he shared his secret place with the future forest ranger, Joseph had been ecstatic and had given Peter a crash course on the unique vegetation of the rare environment.

"Do you realize what a special place this is?"

Peter shrugged. "Well it's special to me. It's my getaway. Nobody knows about it, and I'm never bothered when I'm out here."

"No, I mean I've read about places like this, but never been in one. We are in an ancient swamp with sand dunes and the Atlantic Ocean less than a mile away. This depression is like the kettle ponds the glaciers made here on Cape Cod. But in this case, it's not a pond, it's a swamp. Look, the lower we go, the thicker the growth; broom crowberry and huckleberry disappear, then the ground gets damp and finally we are in a bog. These trees are white cedars, white oaks and a few red maples."

He wondered whatever had happened to Joseph, probably working as a forest ranger in one of the National

Parks. He was thankful to him for his knowledge, but glad he wasn't around to remember Peter's lair. It was his secret refuge.

He put the 2x4s over his shoulder and started into the damp marshy edge of the swamp. Hummocks of dead grass and weeds poked through the murky water. It had been a particularly rainy spring and the water level of the bog was at its highest. Some spots were merely puddles, but in the heart of the mire, black water mixed with decaying vegetation was three feet deep. By the end of a dry summer, the water receded to large puddles, but the spongy footing was tricky and deceiving. It was an inhospitable environment, a breeding ground for mosquitos and insects. Its creepy atmosphere was what attracted Peter. He could picture a druid's or witch's den; he could see Merlin and Arthur lured there by Morgana and Mordred.

After his grandfather had shown him the swamp, he had continued to visit and explored its magical terrain. He would ride his bicycle through the fire roads and the abandoned dirt road. On his second trip, he had found it. In the midst of the soggy bog was a little shelter, a crude fort built by children. He almost missed it. Made with branches, it was covered with rotted canvas that sprouted mold and fungus and provided an unintended camouflage.

As he got older, he had continuously improved the original shabby structure. At fourteen, his grandfather had let him drive the ancient Ford, as long as he stayed off the main roads. Peter had loaded planks of wood, tools, nails and 2x4s, and over the course of two summers built a small shed. Sometimes he pretended he was Robinson Crusoe, marooned in a marsh instead of an island. He imagined talking with his own man "Friday" but was actually glad there wasn't anyone who knew his secret.

Peter knew two paths to his fort. One involved stepping and sometimes jumping from clump to clump. In a few places, the mounds accumulated around the cedar trees so that he stepped and at the same time grabbed the tree for balance. Today, with a stack of wood over his shoulder, he couldn't use that route. He wore his waders, rubber-bib-boots that his grandfather had used for clamming. Even with the boots, you needed to know the safe way through the swamp. Through trial and error and many soggy mistakes, Burke had blazed a shallow path. Today, he wore the rubber waders, combined with a long-sleeve shirt that protected him against mosquitos. However, they also left him soaked in sweat.

Peter was close to his goal. A mossy knoll rose from the fetid waters. It was larger than the other hummocks and looked out of place, yet also blended into the marshy growth. Like an illustration from Grimm's Fairy Tales, it cast a spooky aura. Peter stepped onto the knoll and dropped his load of lumber. He pulled back a cloak of moss that revealed a makeshift door. Beneath his camouflage was a well-crafted shelter. It was roughly eight feet square. Four white cedar trees formed the corner posts, and were the reason it didn't have true right angles. Pine planks fashioned the crude floor, walls and low ceiling. Vines and moss covered the exterior, so it looked part of the natural environment.

He kept thinking about Rachel, the woman of his fantasies. She was in danger, and didn't even know it. That army soldier was dead, one less threat to her safety. Cape Cod was abuzz with the news, and police were swarming over the Outer Cape, asking all kinds of questions. He needed her hidden away for her own protection. He remembered how Helen had been spirited away to Troy for her own good. With Rachel it was the same thing. She needed a champion—not someone brawny and strong, but with the intelligence and sensitivity to take her away from these crass, violent men of her backwater village. He remembered the words of Alexander Dumas from *The Count of Monte Cristo: "Woman is sacred; the woman one loves is holy."*

He looked at the door's combination lock, and found something wrong with it. He examined the area; someone had tried to open the door. Crude efforts had produced dents in the lock, and scratches in the wood around the hasp. Peter scowled in anger. Now he noticed that the moss camouflage had been disturbed as well. This could present a serious problem with his plans. He suspected it was town kids, wild urchins who roamed around unchecked. Like the boys who had bullied him as a child. Well, he would prepare a few surprises for them.

He turned the lock to its three numbers and it snapped open. At least it still worked. Then he ducked through the door into the low one-room hut. A collapsible canvas army cot stood against the left wall. Watertight army surplus crates lined the other sidewall. They were filled with nonperishable food supplies, hard tack crackers, army K rations and containers of water. If the communist Soviet Union and United States launched a nuclear war, this was his bomb shelter, perhaps not safe from radiation, but at least he had uncontaminated food and water.

He opened a toolbox and pulled out a saw, hammer and nails. The 2x4s would make a protective cage around the army cot, a place he could keep Rachel until she understood. It would give him time to explain his plan. She was smart; she would understand. He just had to get her here, and then convince her to stay with him.

The cautious, law-abiding voice in the back of his brain tried to tell him to be careful, that this was a bad idea. Peter pushed the caution aside. He wouldn't listen to that voice anymore. All his life he had obeyed the little voice, and where had it gotten him? No, he listened to a different voice now: A voice that urged action. A voice that spoke like thunder, and repeated passages from his favorite books. The voice of Banquo, advising Macbeth, *"Let every man be master of his time."* It was time to live his life like the bold heroes he idolized. He was ready to put his plan in place.

Chapter 23

Rachel & Elaine – An Awkward Talk
Sunday Evening, July 6th

Rachel pulled into the driveway of the Samuels' house. The weather-beaten shingles of the classic Cape had seen better days. The wood trim showed only random flecks of white paint; the boards were dried, cracked and buckled. Turning off the engine of the old DeSoto coupe, she realized for the first time how awkward this conversation might be.

Elaine was the catalyst who had set in motion the breakup with Rob, and the rash decision to elope with Jimmy. If only Rachel hadn't been sick the night of the going-away beach party! If she had been at the gathering, Elaine never would have had the chance to seduce Rob. At first she had blamed Rob, but later she understood that enticing the most handsome, popular boy in school was more Elaine's style.

She knocked on the flimsy screen door. "Hi, Elaine, It's Rachel Curtis. I need your help. It's about Jimmy and the murder."

The door opened and Elaine motioned her to enter, with an exaggerated sweep of her hand. A lit cigarette dangled from the corner of her mouth, and she squinted as the smoke stung her eyes. She was barefoot with cutoff denim shorts and an old Bound Brook Basketball sleeveless jersey. Even in old clothes, she oozed a sultry allure. "Well, well, a visit from the duchess of Bound Brook. I am honored, even though I know you really didn't come to see me."

Rachel ignored the comment. "You're right, it's about Jimmy. I'm afraid they're going to arrest him for the murder."

"You know I already talked to the State Police, right? I told them everything. That son-of-a-bitch tried to rape me. I don't know who killed him, but it wasn't me and it wasn't Moose. Frankly, whoever did it gave him what he deserved."

"I know that you and Moose didn't do it, and that Jimmy didn't do it either. Jimmy might do something violent to defend himself, but track down a defenseless man? No, it wasn't Jimmy."

"You want to talk with Moose too? You missed him, he just left. He's been staying here, you know. At first I felt like I needed protection, but you know he's really a sweet guy under all that bully stuff." Elaine gave her a wink.

"Oh, well, I . . . well, that's nice. I'm glad for the two of you. I hope things work out."

Elaine took the cigarette and crushed it into a clamshell ashtray. "Listen, I'm sorry about the attitude, but you know it just comes out when I see you. 'Miss Perfect': pretty, smart, athletic, good parents, . . . Well you've got it all, including two of the best guys I ever knew, all gaga over you. I know, I know . . . I screwed things up with you and Rob. But what you did— you know, dumping him . . . then stringing Jimmy along . . . Well, that wasn't my decision, it was yours!"

Rachel's face burned. "You are right, Elaine. I am so far from perfect. I've messed up more than anybody I know, but I can't turn back the clock. What I can do is everything possible to keep Jimmy from going to jail or worse, for something he didn't do. So can we get past our issues with each other? Jimmy needs our help."

Elaine looked away. "Okay, Jim is a good guy and I'll tell you all I can remember about that night."

Rachel took out a small notebook and pen and took notes while Elaine went through the events of the evening.

"So when you were at the pond, or after Moose drove you home, did you see anybody else or any other cars, maybe?"

"No, nobody. But when we got out on Bound Brook Pond Road, before we got to the highway, I think I remember some headlights going past us."

"Some, so more than one, do you remember how many?"

"I wasn't really looking. I just remember the inside of the truck kinda lit up, I think maybe twice. I'm not sure, but must have been some other cars. Where they were going, well, I couldn't tell you. They might have just been going home."

"If you think of anything else let me know. Oh, and do you know anyone who might have had a motive to kill Bowers?"

"I know he was a nasty piece of work, but he was handsome and acted very charming so he could get his own way. Moose told me that Sal Santos was looking for him. It sounds like Bowers might have done the same thing to Liz Santos that he tried to do to me."

"Did you see Sal that night?"

"No, I didn't. That Liz is a real sweet and pretty girl, but she is way too naïve to deal with a creep like Bowers. A few months ago, she was hanging around the Mayflower. I think maybe she and Frankie, the bartender, had a flirtation going. Then she stopped coming by. She acts much younger than she looks, and Sal is protective of her."

Rachel put away the notebook and pen. "Well, call me or Rob if you think of anything else."

Elaine nodded. "I will. Oh, and listen, I'm sorry about giving you all that 'Miss Perfect' stuff. I was always jealous of you, but I have to be honest and say it, you were always nice to me. Even when the other girls all froze me out and whispered behind my back, well, you treated me decently. Want you to know I appreciate it. And, well, I hope things work out with you and Rob."

*****

Jim Curtis sat up on the hard bunk bed of the Provincetown jail. His head hurt, his mouth was dry and his stomach was doing flips; he knew the symptoms of a hangover. He pushed himself to his feet and wobbled as he gained his balance. He was barefoot and dressed only his boxer shorts. He shuffled to the bars of the cell.

"Hello, anybody there? Any chance I can get a drink of water?" The sound of someone moving in the outer room gave him some hope.

"Be there in a minute." A man about his age dressed in a Provincetown police uniform stood in the door opening. "Did you sleep it off yet? I'll get you some water, but if you puke, I swear you'll have to clean it up yourself."

"It'll be okay. Afraid to say I have extensive experience with hangovers. I'm past the puking stage and I'll sip the water slowly."

"Humph . . . we'll see." The guard returned with a paper cup of water.

Jim forced himself to drink it slowly. "So what I am doing here?"

"You don't remember? Shows how drunk you must have been."

Jim squinted and tried to coax a memory from his foggy brain. "I might have a little idea, but maybe you can fill in the blanks for me."

"Well I wasn't there, but from what I hear you were being brought in for questioning about that army murder, and you attacked a state trooper and had to be subdued. When they brought you here, you were totally out of it."

"So is that why I'm here?"

"You are facing drunk and disorderly charges, and being held for questioning about the murder. There might also be assault on a police officer and resisting-arrest charges, but all that is above my pay grade. You're scheduled to be interviewed by the troopers tomorrow. Until they decide if you stay or go, well you are our guest, probably at least a few days. If they press the murder charges, you'll be moved to Barnstable County Jail."

Jim couldn't believe what he had heard.

"Oh, and you've got a lawyer. I'm supposed to call Attorney Snow when you're sober enough to talk with him. It's probably too late to reach him now, so make yourself comfortable. You can see him in the morning."

Jim handed the guard the empty paper cup. Sitting on the edge of the bed, he tried to jog his memory. The last clear recollection he had was drinking at the Old Colony Tap. He had too many beers and by the time he quit he was a little wobbly. Like the night before, he had driven toward the West End to avoid the police traffic stop. He had managed to make it home and stumble into bed. Thank God his mother was still at the Gilmore's. The next morning he vaguely remembered finding a bottle of whiskey hidden away in the back of the kitchen cabinet. He recalled sitting on the pier and then a fuzzy image of Bing Tyler. Then the rest all got hazy.

Chapter 24

"If you judge, investigate"
Lucius Annaeus Seneca

Rob found Moose at the door to the Mayflower. "Hey, Moose, have you got a minute to talk?"

"Hi, Rob, I guess, but if there's a spill or they need me to get stuff from the backroom, then I'll have to stop."

"You probably guessed it's about the murder. They are holding Jimmy for questioning, and I'm afraid they're going to charge him. I know you told the police about what you did that night, but I'm more interested in what happened earlier."

Moose frowned. "So is this official police business?"

"No. Sorry, I should have told you right away. I'm off the police force and doing this on my own. I just need to find who did it, so Jimmy doesn't get framed. Can you start with the beginning of the night?"

"Okay. So far we're not that busy, must be a letup after the holiday. I'll tell what I remember." Moose told Rob all the details of the evening, including what he knew about Bowers.

When he mentioned that Sal Santos had been looking for Bowers, "with murder in his eyes," Rob's attention peaked. "So what was Sal so angry about?"

Moose told him what he knew about Liz and Bowers. "If you want more information, you should ask Frankie. There was a time a little while ago when Liz seemed kind of sweet on him."

Moose went on detailing what he had done that evening. Rob listened with an occasional question. "So, Bowers talked with Brian Francis. I have a hunch I know what that was all about. Then he bought Elaine some drinks, and the two of them left for Bound Brook Pond. You hit Bowers in the solar plexus and knocked the wind out of him. Other than that, did he seem okay?"

"Yes, I just gave him the one hard push. I know I knocked the wind out of him; I could hear it and know what it sounds like. Otherwise, he was fine and the water was less than knee deep."

"Did you see anybody else at the pond, or did you see any cars on the road headed to the pond?"

"Didn't see anyone else at the pond. There were no other cars in the parking lot either. After we left the dirt road to the pond, we passed maybe two other cars on Bound Brook Pond Road. I just vaguely remember the headlights. Couldn't tell you anything about the cars though."

"Moose, I know you didn't kill Bowers, and we both know Jimmy wouldn't do it—I don't care how much he hated the man. So anything, I mean anything you remember, or hear, that could help him, please tell the police, but tell me too."

"Sure thing, Rob."

Rob headed over to the bar and the bartender gave him a nod. "Are you Frankie?"

"Yup. I know you, you're Rob Caldwell. When I was a kid, I used to watch you play basketball against P'town High. Moose was on that team too; man, you were good!"

"Thanks, but listen, can you talk? I'm trying to help with the murder investigation. I've got to tell you, though, it's unofficial. I'm off the police force now."

"What do you need to know?"

"Moose gave me most of what I need, but can you tell me more about Sal Santos and his daughter Liz?"

"Well, I got to be honest with you," Frankie nodded. "A couple of months ago, Liz and I had a little bit of a thing going on. I mean nothing that went very far, a few pecks on the cheek, but that was it. So Sal came to see me. He was very nice, but he asked me to stop seeing her. Liz is really pretty and she's only nineteen. Anyway, she is also a little on the slow side mentally. Not so you would notice it at first; I mean, she's not stupid, just really naïve. So Sal watches her like a hawk. Liz trusts people too much."

"So you stopped?"

"Yes, and it wasn't easy, because I really like her and she kept coming around a few times. I'm sure it hurt her feelings when I broke it off. The thing is, Sal told me his wife is determined to have Liz become a nun. At first he was against it, but now he thinks it would be the best way to protect her."

"So it would have been easy for Bowers to do something to her?"

Frankie's face hardened. "Listen, I'm glad that Bowers creep is dead. What he did to Liz, man, he deserved it. Only wish I did it. Wait . . . I mean . . . I didn't do it, but whoever did should get a medal."

"I get it," Rob nodded. "How do I find Sal Santos?"

"Well, you don't, at least not for a week or so. I heard he went fishing, headed out to George's Bank."

"Interesting timing. What about Brian Francis, where do I find him?"

Frankie laughed. "Funny you should ask. One of the guys came in asking for him about an hour ago. I overheard somebody say that Brian had left town for a while. He's supposed to have some business deal off-Cape. If I know Brian, it will be something shady."

"So two men I need to talk with just happen to disappear."

"What can I tell you? That's life," chuckled Frankie.

Rob looked over the bar and pointed to the baseball bat in the corner. "You ever use that?"

"Never had to hit anybody with it, but a few times it has helped to convince some bad drunks to leave. Why, what are you saying? You think I did it? No such luck. I think this conversation is done."

There was an awkward silence while Frankie seemed to reconsider. "Look, you're going to find out anyway. I told the P'town cops and Tony Oliver had told them he saw me already. After I locked up the bar, I took a ride to Bound Brook Pond."

"What! Now you tell me?"

"But I didn't get there. I was almost there, and then I recognized Moose's truck headed away from the pond. So I figured Moose wouldn't leave unless Elaine was fine. I admit I didn't tell the cops at first, but I went back and gave them the full story."

Rob shook his head. "So what did you do?"

"I turned around in the next driveway I saw and headed home."

"Did you bring the bat with you?"

"No, no. Honest it wasn't like that. I just wanted to make sure everything was okay with Moose and Elaine. Man, I already told the police. I know it makes me a suspect, but look, I saw the scumbag almost every night after he hurt Liz. I had plenty of chances to do something to him. Sure, I was mad. I mean, Liz is such a gentle, sweet girl. I knew Sal would probably take care of things, and well, Sal is her father. Me, I'm just a guy she had a crush on."

"If you did it, and Jimmy takes the fall . . . I'll be coming back to see you."

Frankie motioned him away, turned his back and went to the other end of the bar. Rob threw a pocketful of change on the bar, waved to Moose and went out to the street. It took him a minute to get his composure. Means, motive, opportunity: there was at least another prime suspect.

His next stop was the Old Colony Tap, across the street and only a few doors down from the Mayflower. The O.C.T. was a serious bar. No pretensions and no tourists. Fishnets and lobster pots hung from the walls and there was a lingering odor of fish, sweat and beer. Beneath the hardcore atmosphere was a comfortable place for town regulars.

Rob asked the bartender for Frank Days, the owner.

"Frank ain't in tonight. Don't expect a big crowd, it being Sunday night. It's the one night of the week that a lot of the guys get to spend with the wife and kids. That is, unless they want to take a lot of guff from the old lady. So what can I get you?"

Rob ordered a beer. "I'm asking people about last night. An army guy was murdered; the police probably talked to you."

"Sure, they talked to me. I know the guy that got killed too, but he wasn't in here the last few nights."

"When he did come in, what did he do? Who did he talk with?"

"I mind my own business. I can't have people think that I'm ratting them out for everything I overhear. Hey, I'm a bartender; I'm the psychiatrist for the ordinary people. I think that's some kind of doctor-client privilege, you know, like a priest?"

Rob felt his temper rise. He stood up and got right in the man's face. "Look, buddy, you ain't a doctor or a priest. I need some answers, and I'm not in the mood to waste time. Maybe I need to go back to my truck and get my badge. I just need a few questions answered unofficially, or I can come back and make it official."

The bartender looked up at Rob's six-foot-three frame. "Hey, I didn't know you was a cop. Sure, ask your questions, fire away."

With the bartender's cooperation, Rob learned that Bowers had frequently come in the Old Colony, but never stayed long. He always talked with a few guys the bartender described as "scum." Then they would leave together.

"I do remember that army guy, bragging about how he practically ran that army base. Something about how the army had screwed up and there was just a green lieutenant there and Bowers had to tell him everything to do."

"Was Brian Francis one of the guys Bowers talked with?"

"Yes, and he's one of the people that I don't want to ever know that I told you anything. He knows people that can hurt you."

"He'll never hear anything from me. Do you know what Bowers and Brian Francis talked about?"

"No. . . . Well, wait a minute, one night they were having a really heated talk. They tried to whisper, but I did hear Brian tell Bowers something like, *I don't like to get cheated,* and then he said, *I promised people.*"

"Anything else?"

"No, and I already told you too much."

"OK, we won't talk about them. Do you know Jimmy Curtis?"

"I didn't at first, but then one of the guys told me his name and that he was a war hero." As the bartender went on, Rob learned that Jim had spent the last few nights at the bar, doing serious drinking.

"So Jimmy came in the last two nights, drank a lot, and left around closing time. Did he talk with anyone in particular?"

"Last night he didn't talk with anybody. He was very into his beers. But the night before, would have been the

Fourth, he talked with Mike Tasha. I guess they used to play basketball against each other."

"I know Mike. Yes, he played for P'town. Good kid. So what was Tasha doing here?"

"Like everybody else, came in for a beer and a little conversation. He doesn't come often. You know, that night was the most beers I ever seen him drink. He and that Jimmy guy were reminiscing about old times."

Rob took a last swig from his beer and smacked a five-dollar bill on the bar. "Thanks for your help. I probably won't be back, but if I do, can we skip the attitude next time?"

The bartender scooped the bill. "Sure thing."

*****

Rob got back to the cottage late. The Desoto was in the driveway, so he knew Rachel was there. Curled up on the couch, she was half-asleep. He leaned over and gave her a kiss on the cheek.

"Oh, hi. Sorry, I was just drifting off. How did your night in Provincetown go?"

"You first. Did you learn anything from Elaine?"

"Not really. The only thing new I learned is that she thinks there were maybe two other cars on Bound Brook Pond Road at around two in the morning."

"Moose said the same thing."

Rachel pushed herself up and Rob sat down next to her on the sofa. "Talking to Elaine was really weird. I didn't even think until I got there how hard it might be. You know, with all the history between her and you and me and Jimmy. I mean it was really dredging up the past."

"So was she cooperative?"

"Yes, once we got past the attitude. I never stopped to think about what a hard life she's had. She said something about her being together with Moose, like romantically?"

"Yes, when Skip and I went over there to talk to her, it was obvious that Moose had spent the night. Elaine made it pretty clear that they were sort of a couple."

"Funny, I always had a different feeling about Moose."

"What do you mean?"

She shook her head. "Nothing. Okay, it's your turn tell me about P'town."

He gave her a summary of his talks with Moose, Frankie and the Old Colony Tap's bartender.

Rachel frowned. "So the bartender puts Jimmy across the street from the Mayflower, around the same time that Bowers and Elaine left to go to the pond. Not what I wanted to hear."

"Let me get this straight," she continued, "and tell me if I'm wrong. Let's rule out Moose, Elaine and Jimmy. What I hear is that Sal Santos had a motive and he was looking for Bowers. His daughter got assaulted, and Sal was mad enough to kill him. Then the next day he goes fishing for a week."

"Yup!"

"Then we've got Brian Francis. He was obviously doing crooked deals with Bowers, probably the stolen stuff from the PX. Now, all of a sudden, he leaves town the day after Bowers is murdered. Maybe he and Bowers had a business deal that went bad. If Bowers was about to get discovered, could it be that Brian killed him to keep him quiet?"

"Yes, and then there is Frankie the bartender. He admits that he had a romance with Liz Santos. It sounded to me like he still had feelings. Maybe they are not romantic anymore, but I would say he's still protective. He keeps a baseball bat behind the bar. He admits he headed out toward the pond, but says he turned back when he recognized Moose's truck."

Rachel finished his thought. "So what if he didn't turn around? What if he continued to the pond and clubbed Bowers? Maybe seeing him try to do the same thing to Elaine was just too much for him."

Rob nodded. "He could be lying, and I wish he did it, just to get Jimmy off, but honestly I believe him. Of course when you've been doing MP and police work as long as I have, you learn that some people are really good liars."

"So why isn't he in jail? He sounds like as good a suspect as Jimmy."

"Well, let's see. He didn't threaten to kill Bowers in front of 100 witnesses, and he didn't get drunk and assault a state trooper."

"My point exactly," Rachel chimed in. "Who is stupid enough to do what Jimmy did, if you actually planned to kill Bowers and get away with it? I think it is someone who planned this out a lot better than a drunk Jimmy would have."

"Totally agree, but murder and crime investigations aren't necessarily logical. They probably should be, but they just aren't."

"This is starting to sound like an Agatha Christie novel. You know, like *Murder on the Orient Express*. So many suspects, and then it turns out they all did it together."

"Boy, I wish it was a novel," sighed Rob.

"Tomorrow I'm going to Camp Wellfleet. My father asked me to help at the PX; with Jimmy locked up, they need a hand. I'm going to try to ask around the base while I'm there, and I want to talk with Simon directly."

"I'm heading back to Provincetown tomorrow. I've got a couple of friends on the police force, and I'm going to see if they can get me in to talk with Jimmy.

Rachel snuggled against his chest. "Talking about all this stuff makes me feel sad and angry. It's like seeing the worst side of people."

Rob hugged her tight.

Chapter 25

"Nothing is more deceptive than an obvious fact"
The Adventures of Sherlock Holmes – Arthur Conan Doyle

Monday Morning, July 7th

Rachel and her father arrived at the Camp Wellfleet gate around 7:30 in the morning. George waved to the familiar guard, but the soldier put up his hand for him to stop. "Good morning, sir, I recognize you, but I don't know this young lady. I don't have any permission for her to enter the base."

"She's going to help at the PX. We are shorthanded. James Curtis, one of our workers, won't be coming in and we need to fill the spot. She's my daughter. I can vouch for her."

"Sir, things are a lot tighter now that the National Guard has arrived. Also, I should warn you that with the death of Sergeant Bowers, the new commanding officer is on the warpath. . . . Oh, I really shouldn't have said anything."

"Don't worry, Private. I won't repeat it."

"Thank you, sir. Stay here, I have to call the Officer-on-Duty and see what the new protocol is for you civilians." The soldier stepped into the small guardhouse and made a call. When he finished, he stepped out with a clipboard and two yellow file cards.

"Sir, I need to sign you both in and give you these cards. They are temporary passes for civilians. I have to warn you that they are limited to the PX. Do not go anywhere else on the base. Do you understand? If you do, it would be a serious breach of base security. I will use the same protocol when the other PX workers get here."

"Thank you, Private. Yes, we understand."

George could hardly believe his eyes as he took in the transformation of the army base. On Thursday before the long weekend, it had been a barren patch of sand. There were only a couple dozen soldiers and maybe ten carpenters, with a half-dozen completed buildings and numerous construction projects. Now the camp was buzzing with the activity of a thousand soldiers, military vehicles and mobile artillery pieces. The once-barren expanse of sand was covered with neat rows of two-person pup tents for as far as his eyes could see.

They parked and George unlocked the building. "I appreciate you helping out today. I have no idea how busy we'll be, or even if they are going to let soldiers shop. Let me give you a crash course before Simon and Benny get here."

"Remember, I agreed to do this to help you out, but also to try and get information that could help Jimmy."

"Well, I guess you're not going to be talking to any of the army brass. These passes limit us to staying in the PX."

Rachel gave him a smile. "We'll see."

Around 8 a.m. Simon arrived. "Hi, I thought I was early, but you beat me. You must be Rachel. Thanks for filling in for Jimmy. Boy, I hope it's only temporary. Have you heard anymore?"

Rachel shook her head. "Not much, but it doesn't sound good. In fact, while I'm here I would appreciate it if you would tell me what you can about the thefts. Why did you think it was Bowers?"

Simon explained how he had done a stakeout of the PX that night, and had seen the shadowy figure go inside and then disappear into the trees. "When I reported the theft to the Lieutenant, I met Sergeant Bowers. I think he got the keys before we did. He could have kept one or made a copy. He tried to blame it on the construction workers. Then when I saw him walking away, well, his shape and the way he walked reminded me of the person I saw that night."

"So anything else?"

Simon paused. "No . . . well, yes, there is. I followed Bowers Thursday night. He went to Provincetown. I think that's probably where he was selling the cigarettes and things he stole from here."

"Did you actually see him selling anything?"

"No, just a feeling."

"What about Friday or Saturday, the night of the murder? Did you see anything?"

"No."

"Well, thank you. If you can think of anything that could help Jimmy, please let us know. I'm really afraid for him."

Simon nodded. "Of course. Jimmy is a good worker and a nice guy. I'd hate to see anything bad happen to him." He walked away and headed to the sporting goods section.

Her father had told her about Simon. He was definitely a bit of an "odd duck." Something about their conversation bothered her, though. She couldn't tell if was just Simon being Simon or something else.

The door to the PX opened and an army officer walked in. In a thick southern accent he asked, "Hello, may I speak with the manager?"

"I'm the manager," Simon answered.

"Sir, I'm Captain Ray Anderson. I have the schedule for when the soldiers can use the PX. We won't start until this afternoon. There's too much setting up to do. They'll be coming in one platoon at a time, and they get 20 minutes to shop before the next group comes in."

He handed Simon a printed schedule and then glanced at Rachel. "Oh, who is this lovely young lady?"

Stepping forward, she offered her hand. "Hello, I'm Rachel, George's daughter. I'll be helping out here, at least for now."

"Well, ma'am, pleased to meet you." He held her hand gently. For a moment, Rachel thought he was going to kiss it. "Anything else I can do for you folks, why y'all just let me know."

Rachel saw an opportunity. "Why, thank you, Captain. I must say it is so refreshing to find a southern gentleman here on Cape Cod. I wonder if you would mind clearing up a few things we were wondering about."

"Certainly, ma'am, what would you like to know?"

"Well, I know the man who was killed was a sergeant here, and a man they are questioning worked here in the PX. I just wondered, you know, it must be hard having to deal with that and also setting up an army base practically from scratch."

"Ma'am? Yes, it is challenging, but that's what we train for, you know: to meet the challenges."

"Wasn't it strange that there was only one officer here all of last week? I mean from what I hear Sergeant Bowers practically ran the base."

Anderson looked uncomfortable, but after a pause he answered, "Yes, ma'am, sometimes army paperwork gets messed up. With the war going on, the major emphasis is supporting our troops in Korea, so maybe Camp Wellfleet doesn't get as much attention. But we are up to speed now and fully staffed."

"I suppose Lieutenant Gallant must have told you that somebody was stealing from the PX. Our manager here, Simon, he thinks it was that Sergeant Bowers."

Captain Anderson looked surprised. "Gosh, ma'am, I don't know much about what's going on with the investigation. That is the Colonel's job, but I don't think that would surprise

Colonel Murphy. I guess he knew Sergeant Bowers from before the war, and I got the impression that he didn't trust him. As for Lieutenant Gallant, well, I guess I shouldn't say anything, but let's just say he didn't help his career much."

"Oh well, I don't want anyone to get in trouble."

"No, ma'am, but I do know that y'all will probably be getting some questions from the army CIS about the thefts. I guess the murder is being taken care of by the state police, and the army will investigate the stolen goods."

"Well, thank you, Captain. I'm sure it'll get sorted out."

"Yes, ma'am, and if there is anything I can do for you, why, all you do is ask. I must say it's nice to see that Alabama doesn't have all the pretty girls."

Rachel reddened. "Thank you!"

"Ma'am, I was thinking, you know I've never been to Cape Cod before, and well maybe sometime you could show me around?"

"Well, Captain Anderson, I'll think about that."

Anderson smiled. "Gentlemen and Miss Rachel, it's been a pleasure. I should be getting back to my duties. Oh, one more thing. We start artillery practice soon. It can get pretty loud."

Captain Anderson left and Benny Brown just started laughing. George Gilmore shook his head. "My daughter the actress. I wish your mother could have seen that."

Rachel smiled and did a curtsy. "Well y'all, sometimes a girl's got to do what a girl's got to do."

*****

"Rob, how did you get in here?"

Rob winked at Jim. "Sometimes it helps to have friends in key places. Listen, I don't have long, so let's cut right to the chase. Tell me what I can do, or who I need to talk to."

"I talked to my lawyer about an hour ago. He consulted with a criminal law specialist out of Boston. Unless I get charged with the murder, they agree that Attorney Snow can represent me best for now. We are waiting for the State Police or DA to do a formal interview today."

"Well, I have some news on that. It might be delayed. I just heard that the lead State Trooper, Don Stewart, had a death in the family. He'll be at his grandmother's services in Falmouth for a day or two. It means you might be here longer, but maybe we can learn more by then."

"Well, I've been in worse situations. It's better than a foxhole in Korea, I guess."

"What can you tell me that can get you out of here?"

Jimmy sighed. "Probably nothing the police, you and everybody else doesn't already know. My lawyer thinks he can get me out of here. They don't have any real evidence, all just circumstantial. Just the fact that I had a fight with the man, then threatened to kill him, and that I was in Provincetown the same night.

"I don't know if there is such a thing as a *"too drunk"* defense, but he might try it. I barely remember driving home. Lucky I didn't kill someone then, but it wouldn't have been Bowers. That man was a skilled soldier. You would have to have your wits about you to kill him. In fact, if I tried it while I was drunk, he probably would have killed *me*."

Rob patted Jim's shoulder. "Well, I just want you to know that Rachel and I are doing everything we can to find the real killer and get you out of here."

"I don't deserve friends like you two."

"Stop, you sell yourself short. Why don't you think you deserve our help?"

"I've had time to think in here; nothing else to do. I was doing pretty good, until Bowers showed up. Biggest thing was I stayed off the bottle. Then things happened: my two flat tires, our shed burning down, and then Bowers shows up at the baseball game and gropes Rachel. I know he did all those things, it had to be him."

"Why would he do all that to you?"

"The man was evil. Oh, he was a hell of a soldier, I'll give him that. But Bowers did something bad to a young Korean girl. Another sergeant told me about it, and said he was going to turn Bowers in. Then, surprise, surprise, that sergeant ends up dead the next day. Can't prove it, but I don't give the Chinese credit for that one."

"What's that got to do with you?"

"The brass got a complaint from the girl's father; guess he had connections. They came to me and I told them what I knew. I heard that Bowers got busted in rank, and shipped back stateside. Now we know where—small world. Bowers didn't take anything lying down. I guess he blamed me."

"I hope your lawyer told you to be careful what you say."

"Yes, I probably shouldn't even be telling you all this, in case someone is listening."

"Okay, well if you think of anything I should know, get word to the guard named Arthur. He'll pass it on to me."

"Rob, don't go yet. Can you stay until they kick you out? I have some things I need to get off my chest."

"Sure thing."

"I'm really scared that even if I get out of this, I'm going to screw up again. It's the drinking; I thought I had it licked, but it hangs on to me and won't let go. Seeing Bowers triggered it all over again. It's funny what I thought about, though. I thought about you and Rachel, not Bowers or Korea. I know we were great friends, all of us, but I never told you how jealous I was. You were the best at everything. The best athlete, the best student, and you had Rachel. To make it worse you are too damn nice to hate," he laughed. "How's that for a criticism: too nice?"

"Jimmy, you were a terrific guard in basketball, made the All-Star team, and everybody in school liked you and looked up to you. I might have had better book smarts than you did, but that doesn't help much out in life. Look what you did in the army."

"I know, it isn't logical, it's just how I feel. I feel like a screw up. Except in the army. In the army I didn't have to compete with you. I was out of your shadow, and I guess the kind of smarts I have do pay off in combat. As a defensive guard in basketball I always watched the other player's eyes, not where he was looking, because that could be a fake. No, I watched his eyes to see what he was thinking; I tried to get in his brain. I think war is like that."

"You were the best defensive player in the league, no question."

"Thanks, Rob. You know, like George Patton said, *the goal of war isn't to die for your country, it's to make the other bastard die for his.* That was my goal: to try to keep my men alive. You know, too many kids watch John Wayne movies. Half the time he dies a glorious death in the end. Well, I've seen too many deaths, and there is nothing glorious about it. Don't get me wrong, I'll die for my country if I have to. But we both know John Wayne is coming back in another movie. In real war, it don't work like that."

Rob shook his head. "Jimmy, you've seen the real thing. I spent the first half of the war organizing shipping convoys and playing basketball for the navy's Newport base team. When I got to the real war in France, it was as an MP rounding up drunk sailors."

The sound of a bang on the bars broke the mood. "Hey, Rob, you need to go. Make it quick before the next shift gets here."

"Will do, Arthur, and thanks."

Rob and Jim stood up and shook hands. "We'll get you out of here, Jim. Then afterwards I'm going to be there for you. We'll get you some help. You might not know this, but Hoopy sees a doctor sometimes. He says it helps with his war memories."

"Thanks, Rob. I don't deserve your help."

"Yes, you do."

Jim laughed. "See I told you so, too damn nice."

Chapter 26

"Hell is empty and all the Devils are here"
William Shakespeare – The Tempest: Act 1, Scene 2

Monday, July 7th

It was late afternoon, and Peter was both excited and angry. He had spent the day working on the swamp hideout. He had strung wires attached to warning bells that would alert him to the approach of any people. The thin wires were about ankle high and he wrapped them around tree trunks, across some of the most obvious paths. The wires should trip any intruders who didn't watch their steps, and give him advance warning.

He was pleased with his results, but irritated that it had caused him to waste most of the day. The work along with a visit to the hardware store had taken hours. Now he didn't have time to get to his grandfather's house in Truro before he checked on Rachel. In his surveillance of her house, he had learned that the father often left very early. That morning Peter had arrived before 7 a.m. but found the driveway near her house occupied. Probably summer people down for the month. So he found another spot that was inconspicuous.

Around 7:15, Rachel and her father appeared. He followed them to the entrance of Camp Wellfleet. That was interesting because the army base was about a mile from the swamp. He waited on the side of the road not far from the base, to make sure Rachel wasn't just dropping off her father. After thirty minutes, he decided she must be staying. By then the hardware store was open and he was able to get to work on his warning trip-wires and bells.

Now the afternoon was getting late, so Peter picked his way through the swamp and back to the Jeepster. He drove another dirt road that came out on Route 6 and then turned south toward Camp Wellfleet. It was 4 p.m. and he knew it might be a long wait, but he didn't want to miss his chance. He needed an opportunity to get Rachel alone. If it wasn't today, then he would go to Truro and get his grandfather's shotgun, .38 revolver, .22 rifle and ammunition. The signs of intruders at his hideout presented a danger he could not ignore. If his chance came to snatch her tonight, then he would have to go to Truro tomorrow.

He knew that today he was crossing a boundary, perhaps risking it all for the chance that Rachel would listen. The little voice told him it was crazy *(wisely, and slow. They stumble that run fast)*, but Peter was done listening to it. All it had ever done was keep him from living his dreams. Now that voice was fading, as another spoke louder. This voice told him it was time. Time to step up and live his life boldly. The words of Hamlet resonated: *"Conscience doth make cowards of us all."* If he didn't take risks, he would never fulfill his destiny. He might never have a chance like this again. He could sit back and let this challenge slip away or, for once in his life, take action.

A vehicle leaving the Camp Wellfleet's entrance caught his eye. It was her father's car and he could see two people in it. They turned onto Route 6 heading toward Bound Brook and Peter followed at a safe distance. The sedan continued to the town center and pulled over to the curb across from the Bound Brook Pharmacy, where Rachel jumped out, closed the car door and waved to her father. Wearing yellow pedal-pusher pants and a white short-sleeve blouse, she took Peter's breath away.

He turned into the back entrance to the Town Hall parking lot and circled back to Main Street. A car pulled out of a space in front of the pharmacy and Peter grabbed the spot. He could see the back of Rachel's head through the store's display window. He waited a minute before he went into the Pharmacy. Tall shelves filled with medications and cosmetics blocked his view, but he could hear her voice.

"Hi, Mr. Williams, how was your holiday weekend?"

"It was good, Rachel. We went over to the neighbor's for a cookout and tossed horseshoes. I wish you were still working here. A lot of people come in asking for you. Any chance I can lure you back for the summer?"

"Oh, well, I miss the place, but right now I'm helping my father at the Camp Wellfleet PX. I'm sure you heard about the murder. You must know that one of the suspects is Jimmy, and they've got him in jail in P'town. We might be getting a divorce, but he's still my friend, and right now I'm trying to help clear his name."

"I heard. It doesn't sound like something Jim would do. I've known him his whole life, and I would vouch for him. Meanwhile, what can I get for you?"

"Nothing right now. I came in to say hello, but also to ask you to keep your eyes and ears open. I know how people gossip and talk in here, without thinking if anyone is listening. Well, if you hear something that might help us find the real killer, please tell me or Rob. Okay?"

"Sure, Rachel. How is Rob?" Williams gave her a wink.

She laughed. "You are still a teaser! Rob is fine. I'm meeting him later at Agnes's."

"Well, say hello for me."

She waved and headed down the center aisle toward the door.

"Rachel, is that you?" She turned to the left and saw Dr. Burke standing by the stationery paper products. "Funny, but I thought I might run into you this summer. I'm at my grandfather's in Truro and I come over here for most of my shopping."

"Oh, hello, Dr. Burke."

"Please call me Peter, we're not at BU now. Listen, can I buy you a cup of coffee?"

Rachel's thoughts raced. She still felt uncomfortable around him, but this might be the best time to explain her situation. He seemed to think she was single and interested in him. She'd better set the record straight.

"Okay, but just a coffee. I'm meeting my boyfriend at Agnes' in about an hour."

Peter smiled. "Well, perfect. We'll get a coffee, we can chat, I'll head home and then you can meet him."

Next door at Agnes' he led her to a table for two near the back. "Hardly anyone here, but this will give us privacy to talk when people start to come in." He pulled the chair out for Rachel and then sat down himself. He could see his car through the window. Honestly, he could not have planned it better.

"Dr. Burke, I mean Peter, there's something I need to tell you before we talk any further."

"Sure, Rachel, what is it?"

She spoke quickly. "First, I am Mrs. Curtis not Miss Curtis. Technically, I am still married to James Curtis. I'm not sure if you heard about the murder, but Jimmy is being questioned about it. Anyway, that has nothing to do with what I needed to say. So, our divorce should be final fairly soon, and you should know I have a serious relationship with Rob, my boyfriend, the man I'm meeting."

Peter maintained his composure. Sometimes he found it easier if he assumed the identity of one of his favorite characters, for this situation perhaps an English gentleman from Dickens or Austen would suffice. Someone suave and debonair.

"Why, Rachel, I think that is wonderful. So pleased that you're finding someone new."

"Thank you . . . uh, Peter."

Had she heard him correctly? Something in his voice and manner seemed to have changed.

"So, Rachel, that brings me to why I want to talk with you."

"Hey, you two want anything?" yelled a voice from behind the counter. "We don't start regular table service until five."

"Sure, Agnes, just two hot coffees, I think."

Peter nodded.

"Comin' right up."

Peter stood up. "I'll get these." He walked to the counter and watched Agnes pour two steaming hot mugs. He turned to Rachel. "How do you take it?"

"Two sugar cubes and milk, thanks."

Agnes handed him the two mugs and pushed the sugar and milk containers toward him. He pulled out two dollars and left them on the counter. "Keep the change."

"Thank you," replied Agnes.

Peter added two lumps of sugar and poured in some milk. Then he used his body to block what he did next. His right hand reached into his pocket and unscrewed the cap from a small vial of liquid. Leaving the cap in his pocket, he extracted the vial and cupped it with his hand. While he stirred the milk and sugar, he slipped the liquid into the coffee.

Chloral nitrate; his grandfather had used it. Just a drop helped grandpa get a good night's sleep. More than a little and it was a "Mickey Finn" or "Knockout Drops."

He brought the coffees back to the table. "Here you go. Drink some, and tell me if I did it right." He sat down and sipped his black coffee while Rachel drank hers. "Yes, it's fine, thanks again."

"You are welcome. Let me tell you what I was thinking." His voice took on a clipped, cultured tone. "You are far too bright and talented not to make use of your abilities. When classes start in the fall, I'll speak to the department chair. I am sure I can get you a teaching assistant position. Maybe not until second semester, but when I show the chair your writing, well, it should be easy. He has already talked to me about getting an assistant professor position. Even as a regular instructor, I'm entitled to having a TA. You know, they reduce your tuition for helping me to read and grade papers. Then when you graduate . . ."

"Wait," Rachel raised her hand. "Thank you for the offer, but I'm not even sure I'm going to continue going to school."

Peter put his coffee down. "What? Now I am shocked. Why wouldn't you? I mean, I love Cape Cod for a summer vacation and you can still take July and August off if you want. But really, what is there here for a brilliant woman like you?"

Rachel drank more coffee. "It may be hard to explain to someone like you who's a college professor. I love my boyfriend. We were high school sweethearts, and we never should have broken up. As far as college goes, well, I never had a chance to go before, and I think I wanted to prove to myself that I could do it. Now, I want to stay here in Bound Brook, and I don't need a college degree to get a decent job here. I think I would just be wasting three or four more years."

Peter knew his decision was made for him. If Rachel had been open to his idea, he would have knocked over her coffee (*oh, clumsy me!*). She would be feeling a little off and he could drive her home or she could wait for the boyfriend. But now he had crossed the Rubicon. He was committed to his plan.

"Nothing to say?" she asked.

"Well, I am disappointed. I thought you had more ambition than the tedious people who live here."

Rachel's face turned red. "Tedious people. What are you, are some intellectual snob? My boyfriend has a degree in English from Brown University; that's the Ivy League, I think you know. My father is a school principal with his degree from Tufts and a Masters from BU. As for the rest of the people who live here, well, for them, degrees don't mean a thing. They are happy doing what they want to do. They live in a paradise and they don't need a Ph.D. to enjoy it."

She took a last chug of her coffee and slammed down the mug. "I think this conversation is over!"

"Wait . . . I am so sorry. I know that came out wrong. I didn't mean to insult your friends, or the people who live here. It's just that you have so much intellectual potential. You could be a professor yourself, and your boyfriend could come with you."

Rachel took a deep breath. She felt a little dizzy. "I'm still thinking about it. I haven't decided for sure, but I wanted you to know that there is a good chance that I'm not going back to school." Her words seemed slurred and it was an effort to form her thoughts. "Also, I was getting the feeling . . . well . . . that you thought . . . you know . . . that maybe I liked you . . . and . . . and . . . I don't feel good . . . I think I'm going to faint."

Peter stood up. "Here let me help you. My car is outside. I'll take you home right away." He took Rachel by the arm and she wobbled to her feet. "Oh, Miss Agnes, the lady is not feeling well, I'm going to drive to her house."

"Rachel, sweetie, are you alright?"

"She'll be fine, probably the heat. I'll scoot her right home."

Rachel was slumped against him as he opened the door and helped her outside. He got her into the Jeepster with some effort.

"Where . . . we . . . going?" Those were the last words she said.

Agnes watched them drive away. Then she turned to the telephone. "Hello, George?" She told him what had happened, and to expect Rachel to arrive soon.

Chapter 27

Missing

"Hi Agnes, I'm meeting Rachel, she should be here any minute."

"Geez, Rob, you missed her already."

"What are you talking about? She said to meet her at five."

"Well, she was with some dandyish young man. They had some coffee, talked and then she wasn't feeling well, so he said he would drive her home."

"How long ago was that?"

"They must have left 25 or 30 minutes ago. I called George and said he should expect her."

The phone rang. "Hello, George, hmm . . . what do you mean, she didn't get home yet? She should have been there by now."

Rob reached for the phone. "Here, Agnes, can I speak with George?"

"Hi, George, it's Rob. I just got here. I was supposed to meet Rachel. I know . . . I know. Listen, let me talk to Agnes and see if we can figure out who this mystery man is. I'll call you if we get anywhere, and you call here if she shows up. Yup, Yup, okay." He hung up the phone.

He kept his hand on the receiver, then picked it up and dialed. Agnes could hear the phone ringing at the other end.

"Well, she's not at my house, or at least she's not answering the phone. Agnes, tell me everything you can about what happened."

She told him step-by-step the details of them coming in for coffee.

"What else can you tell me about the man?"

"He seemed good looking, maybe late twenties, wore long pants and a long-sleeve shirt, but very lightweight material. He wore a big floppy hat and kept it in on, even here inside. It kept me from getting a real good look at this face. It was weird. He almost dressed like he was going on safari, or maybe like I've seen those beekeeper people. Like he was trying to keep the sun or the bugs away."

"Could you hear what they talked about?"

"Yes, they were talking about college. I heard Rachel say she might not go back. Then they had words, not a big argument, but definitely a disagreement. Then all of a sudden, he said Rachel was feeling ill and he was going to drive her home. She had trouble walking when they left; he half carried her. That's why I called George."

"Did you see his car?"

"Sure did, it was parked right out front. It was a convertible, but different. It almost looked like a Jeep, but different, more sporty. The top was down and it was a dark color, I think maybe maroon?"

"What else can you tell about the man?"

"I don't ever remember seeing him before. One thing, he spoke funny. A little like a proper Bostonian, almost like he was English, but not quite."

The phone rang again and Rob grabbed it. "She's still not home? I was hoping you were calling to say she was there. . . . Sure, let me tell you what I know." He repeated what he had learned from Agnes.

"No, George, you stay there in case she shows up. Call Doc Carter; maybe he took her there because she got too sick. Okay? When I leave here I'm going to drive to my house and make sure she isn't there. It could be she didn't answer the phone because she was sound asleep. Yes, if we don't locate her, I'll take care of talking to Chief Foster. I've got a description of the car. It sounds like one of those fancy Jeeps."

Rob hung up. A memory flashed through his mind. "Agnes, you said they had coffee? Did you serve it? Is it gone?"

"I just poured the coffee. The man came to the counter and got the mugs. He fixed Rachel's for her. I remember she said two cubes and milk. I already cleaned the mugs. Why do you ask?"

"Do you remember how much she drank from her coffee?"

"Yes, his was half full, but her cup was empty."

Rob's mind went back to his navy years. He had spent years as an MP policing sailors' bars in Newport, Rhode Island and Marseille, France. Some sleazy bars specialized in slipping unsuspecting sailors a "Mickey Finn," and then robbing them before tossing them out the backdoor.

"Rob, you're giving me a bad feeling. Is she going to be okay?"

"She better be. Listen, I'm going to drive to my house. I'll call you when I get there, and let you know if she's there or not."

*****

Rob pulled into his shell driveway within ten minutes of leaving the restaurant. No Rachel. He grabbed his phone and called the Police Dispatch. "Hello, Diane, It's Rob. I am afraid we have a serious problem."

He explained the basics and asked her to radio the neighboring police departments to be on the lookout for a car matching Agnes' description. After he hung up, he sat down at the kitchen table. His mind raced, emotions battled logic, anger fought with making plans. What should he do next? He was not going to lose Rachel again.

The phone rang. "Hello, George? She's still not home? Okay, I'll listen."

George spoke. "Maggie just remembered a conversation she had with Rachel that really disturbed her." He went on to relate his daughter's concern about her college teacher. "Rachel seemed uneasy about it, but Maggie said it struck her as more serious than Rachel realized. Maggie remembered that she said something about this teacher having a house on the Cape somewhere near here, but she didn't say where."

"George, I'm going to call Hoopy and Howie Proctor. They both have gas stations, and whoever this guy is, he has to buy gas. I'll ask them to call all the service stations they know. I'll have my cousin Ben call all the other plumbers and electricians he can think of. Maybe this man had some work done and they'll remember that car. Call all the contractors you can think of, and ask them to spread the word about a maroon convertible that is like a Jeep. Somebody must have seen it."

Chapter 28

"So fair and foul a day I have not seen."
William Shakespeare – Macbeth: Act 1, Scene 3

Monday Night , July 7th

One eye fluttered open. Rachel saw dim light. A kerosene lantern cast an amber glow on an unfamiliar scene. She raised her head and struggled to make sense of her surroundings, but the effort made her dizzy. There was a presence close by that she sensed rather than saw.

"Where am I?"

"Finally. Welcome back, Sleeping Beauty!"

Rachel knew that voice. "Dr. Burke, what did you do to me?"

"I didn't do anything. I just feel it's time we had a long talk about your future, and how I can help you."

She tried to understand her physical position. She was on her right side; her face and right eye pressed into something that felt like a coarse pillow. Her knees were pulled up toward her body and she couldn't move her arms.

"Did you tie me up?"

"Well, it was partly to make it easier for me to carry you here."

Panic and adrenaline forced the cobwebs from Rachel's brain. She pushed herself to a sitting position and surveyed her environment. At first, she thought she was in a cave, but then she saw the walls and ceiling were boards. The whole place was small, maybe no more than eight feet square and perhaps five feet high. She was seated on a collapsible canvas cot, her wrists and ankles tied with cotton sash cord.

Then something else registered. "Am I in a cage?"

"Just something to keep you from doing anything rash."

She was encased in a prison with bars of wooden 2x4s. "Have you completely lost your mind? What on earth do you think you are doing? Is this some kind of joke?"

Peter raised his hand as if to halt her. "See, that's why I need to keep you here. At first it will be a shock, but after we talk and you see the logic of my plan, well, then it will all make sense."

"It'll make sense, are you kidding me? You kidnapped me after somehow drugging me, dragged me into a little shack, tied me up and put me in a cage, but it will all make sense. You have completely lost your mind."

He pursed his lips in a pout. "Insulting me won't help."

"Well, tell me what will help, because I need to get out of here."

"Are you thirsty?"

"Yes, but wait . . . I'm not drinking anything you give me. Oh, I get it. It was the coffee, wasn't it? You fixed my coffee and you put something in it."

She stood up, and banged her head on the low ceiling. She twisted her wrists and struggled against the rope.

"You'll only make it hurt. I know how to tie knots. My grandfather taught me."

Rachel stopped and inhaled. This was going to take more than yelling at him. She sat down on the cot. "If I listen to your explanation, will you let me go?"

"That depends. You need to listen and understand."

"Okay, I'm listening."

Peter was sitting on the wooden floor with his back against the opposite wall. He leaned his head forward. "For thousands of years, writers have recorded the fundamental facts of human existence. We delude ourselves. We think we are

modern people and superior to those of older times. The truth is
that mankind's nature has never changed. There are good
people and there are evil people. Oh, I know it's a little more
complicated, but essentially that's it. You are surrounded by
violent, evil men."

"Dr. Burke, I mean Peter, this is not one of your lectures
about classic literature. We're talking about you committing a
crime."

"I thought you were going to listen."

"Yes, yes, I'll listen."

"I saw you get attacked by that man at the baseball
game. That is not something I can let happen again. Couldn't
you feel that man's evil oozing from his pores? Well, now there
is one less evil person in the world."

"What did you do? Did *you* kill him? Was it you?"

"Many a good hanging prevents a bad marriage."

"You're going to quote Shakespeare to me now?"

"Very good. See how intelligent you are?"

"Oh Peter, this has gone too far, you need to stop . . ."

Peter put up his hand again. "I continue . . . The men in
your life are not worthy of you. I know you said your boyfriend
is an Ivy League graduate, but there is more to becoming a
good person than a degree. You deserve better. In ancient
times, there were heroes. Now, I'm not trying to say I am
Achilles, but ordinary men have risen to the challenge before.
They have stepped up to protect the fair women of the world."

Rachel shook her head, but bit her tongue.

"I see you are skeptical. My father was an evil man. Oh,
he was well-educated and made money, but he was cruel and he
drank too much. My mother was trapped and she couldn't cope.
She was depressed and retreated to her bedroom. I wanted to
save her, but I was too little, scrawny and weak.

"Thank God for my grandfather. My father shipped me to Truro every summer, where I lived with my mother's father. My grandfather had his faults. He wasn't educated, and sometimes he also drank too much, but he was the smartest man I ever met. He taught me to hunt, fish, make traps, use tools and build things. He knew that life was cruel, and to survive you had to be prepared."

Peter now stood up, hunching over to avoid hitting his head on the low ceiling. "Don't get me wrong, my grandfather believed in education. He encouraged me to read all the books that I love. Sometimes he asked me to read them to him. He really liked the *Iliad*. He wanted me to read those books, because they taught me the lessons of life.

"You are an exceptional person, Rachel, one in a million. I knew when I met you that we had a special connection. We need to form a partnership. I know you don't love me yet, but perhaps in time you will appreciate how good we can be for each other. *The course of true love never did run smooth.*"

Rachel sighed.

"You may scoff at me quoting literature, but don't you see? The classics are the guide to how we should live our lives. Why is it a crime to stop evil in the world? Does evil deserve the same protections as good? All my life I have over thought my actions. Being an intellectual can tie your hands if you let it. Now I see it: follow the words literally. Hamlet said, *"For there is nothing either good or bad, but thinking makes it so."*

"Peter, don't you see the contradiction? You said that the world comes down to good versus evil. Now you say there is neither good nor bad."

He clenched his fists. "Stop! . . . You still have much to learn. Of course there is good and evil, but what Hamlet is saying is that we overanalyze. That is what I have done all my life; I explained away the people that rejected me. I thought they were right and I was wrong. Now I have seen the truth: they are evil, and I will not bow down to them any longer. They will not rule me."

He spat out his next words, *"Revenge should have no bounds."*

Rachel sat down on the cot, her head slumped to her chest. She couldn't look at this madman, for fear he would read her thoughts. He was crazy, something had snapped. Nothing rational was going to get her out of her prison. She took a breath. "So what now, Peter?"

"We stay here for as long as it takes. I have food and water to last us for weeks. There's a basin in the corner for you to use when . . . well, you know. I won't look."

She looked up. "Peter, people will know I am missing; they will come looking."

"Let them, I'll be ready. Now try to get some sleep. What I gave you is harmless, but it will leave you a little groggy for a while. When you are thinking clearer, things will make more sense. I'm turning off the lantern now. You need to rest."

Rachel looked around the confined space, trying to memorize the details before it was all dark. A dark, reddish brown spot on one of the 2x4 bars caught her eye. "Is that blood? Oh my God, did you club the Sergeant with that? Peter, you have gone too far."

"What are you talking about? It's my blood, nicked my finger with the saw." He waved his left hand in the air.

She trembled with frustration and pent-up anger. Her fury took its toll on her helpless body. Her mind wanted to shut down and sleep, anything to escape the reality of her captivity. It was the drug . . . He was right . . . She felt a growing listlessness. She lowered her head to the pillow and curled into the fetal position. Then the light faded and all was black.

*****

Peter sat in the gloomy darkness and listened to Rachel's soft breathing. Perhaps two hours had passed, two hours filled with excitement. He liked this new Peter, not like the old version: timid, awkward and full of doubt. *Our doubts are traitors and make us lose the good we oft might win by fearing to attempt.*

He knew he should be tired, but his body was running on adrenaline, as exhilaration fired his thoughts. He had more to do tonight. His new boldness had led to a few mistakes. He needed to go to his grandfather's house in Truro, but now they might be looking for him. The restaurant lady had looked out the window and gotten a good view of his uncommon vehicle.

He was ready, filled with impatience to prove his superiority to the authorities. He remembered Robinson Crusoe: *"Fear of danger is ten thousand times more terrifying than danger itself."* He cupped his hand over the flashlight, snapped it on, and in the dim light softly left the cabin. Once outside, he closed the door, slipped the combination lock through the hasp and clicked it shut. His flashlight lit the way as he picked his path, avoiding his trip-wires and bells. With any luck, he would be back before dawn, and Rachel would still be asleep.

*****

Rachel heard him leave. When she had awakened, perhaps thirty minutes before, she had pretended that she was still asleep. It was now or never. She had no idea how long he would be gone, but it might be her only chance.

She had been working her wrists and hands around, pulling and then contracting the thick cotton rope. She hoped Peter had made a mistake in using sash cord that could stretch and loosen the knots. Now she sat up and tested her bindings; they seemed looser. She put her wrists to her mouth, bit her teeth into the knot and twisted her head back and forth. In the dark she only had the sense of touch and intuition.

The piece of rope moved; she pulled her head back and the cord went with it. The tightness around her wrists eased. She relaxed her hands, trying to make them softer and thinner as she pulled her left hand out of the trusses. It was moving. She tucked her thumb inside her palm and suddenly she was free.

Next, she untied her ankles and stood up from the cot. It was made of canvas, stretched over a wooden frame of one-inch square posts and attached with staples. She pushed the front edge of the cot toward the wall and it collapsed. Then she felt her way toward the front-end legs that supported it. Rachel sat on the long side posts, tucked her knees up to her chest, then kicked out against the shorter leg posts. She heard a tearing sound, as the wood moved and the canvas tore away from the staples. She moved to her knees and yanked one of the legs free; now she had a crowbar.

Peter had made another mistake: he had nailed the 2x4s together instead of using screws. Rachel reached the wooden leg out through the bars and then tucked its end back inside the next lowest 2x4. Then, using the upper bar as the fulcrum, she pulled her "crowbar" back toward her and . . . nothing moved. She planted her left foot against the 2x4, leaned back and pulled her makeshift tool with all her strength as she pushed with her foot.

There came the creaking groan of nails pulling free from wood. She fell back as the crowbar moved and her foot pushed the prison bar. It worked. She repeated the process on another 2x4, until she had enough room to squeeze out of her confinement.

She felt her way forward toward to the spot where she had last seen the lantern. Her fingers felt the cool metal base, then she groped until they touched the little box of matches. Rachel struck a match, turned the valve on the kerosene and lit the lantern. She crawled toward the door and pushed; of course it was locked. A metal toolbox caught her eye and she scurried to it. *Eureka!* Hammers, big and small, several types of saws and—yes, an ax, more of a small hatchet. There was even a metal pry-bar, like a small crowbar. She was getting out of here.

Chapter 29

"The fool doth think he is wise,
but a wise man knows himself to be a fool."
William Shakespeare - As You Like It:
Act 5, Scene 3

Pre-Dawn, Tuesday, July 8th

It was close to 2 a.m. before Peter got to his
grandfather's house in the backwoods of Truro. It seemed like
it had taken forever to get from the swamp to the house.
Navigating the dirt roads at night was slow work. The fire road
behind the swamp connected to the Old Kings Highway, which
had been the main thoroughfare in horse and buggy days. It
traveled past Gull and Higgins Ponds across the Herring Run
and eventually connected to Collins Road in Truro.

He crept out onto South Pamet and around Ballston
Beach, past the old cranberry bog. This was tricky, because
these were town roads with regular traffic. He was lucky and
didn't see a single car. Then he turned back onto the unpaved
Old Kings Highway toward Longnook Beach, past the spooky
house of Ozzie Ball and his sister Mary. Finally, he took a left
down a shrub-sheltered driveway and drove another two
hundred yards to a small half-Cape nestled in a hollow of
linden trees.

His grandfather was Herman Higgins, known as Hermie
or H.H. to most people. A few called him Hermit Higgins for
his reclusive ways, but nobody called him that to his face. Peter
was past the point of second thoughts. He remembered the
words of Alexander Dumas: *"Life is a storm, my young friend.*
You will bask in the sunlight one moment, be shattered on the

rocks the next. What makes you a man is what you do when the storm comes." The Count of Monte Cristo spoke to him, bolstering his resolve.

He was at the house to get his grandfather's shotgun, .22 rifle and .38 revolver. The revolver was from Higgins' young days as a Truro special police officer. It was from before Peter had been born, but he took great pride knowing his grandfather had once upheld law and order. There were rumors that Hermie had been dismissed after he had pistol-whipped a selectman's son, breaking up a drunken beach party that had gotten out of control. Peter was sure the act was justified, and one more example of the corruption of powerful people.

The house had no electricity or indoor plumbing and he avoided lighting a lantern. With his flashlight, he went to the bedroom closet, removed the weapons and laid them on the old four-poster bed. Next, he reached up to the closet shelf and took down boxes of shotgun shells and .22 and .38 caliber bullets. In the kitchen, he found an old potato sack and filled it with the revolver and ammunition boxes. Now he was prepared to defend himself and his lady.

*****

It took Rachel longer than expected to chop through the door with the lightweight hatchet. She concentrated on the middle right-hand edge, where she suspected the lock would be located. Eventually, she had created a hole and now heard the ring of the hatchet on metal. She widened the opening until she could see the crosspiece of the lock's hasp. When the space grew to a few inches, she used the blunt end of the hatchet as a hammer, banging down on the metal. It loosened, but wouldn't break free, so she used the small crowbar from the toolbox to pry the hasp. Finally, she took one more blow with the hammer-side of the hatchet and the screws pulled out.

She grabbed the lantern and pushed open the door. The lamp glow only extended a few feet and it took her eyes a minute to adjust. What she saw puzzled her and gave a sick feeling in the pit of her stomach. She was in a marshy place; standing on squishy moss, the light reflecting off watery patches broken up by dark clumps of what she assumed was land. *Where am I*, she wondered, *and which is the way out?* She forced her breathing to slow down and racked her memory for clues. Then it came to her.

When she had rambled the woods with Rob, Hoopy and Jimmy as thirteen-year-olds, they had teamed up with a couple of South Wellfleet boys a few times. The boys, one of the Pierce kids and a Paine boy, had shown them a swamp, near the old Marconi Site. It was an eerie place and she would have been scared to death if she wasn't with the pack of boys.

Now she knew where she was, but which way to get out? The backwoods of South Wellfleet were largely deserted. Heading east would bring her to the ocean, but it might be miles from any help. North would eventually lead to the General Store, which would be closed, and west would get her to Route 6, but that was a hike. South! That was the way; the new army base should only be about a mile, and there would be soldiers on guard duty. So, which direction was south?

She raised the lantern, and in the dim light, inspected the tree trunk that formed one of the corner posts of the shelter. Her left hand felt around the trunk until she stroked the fuzzy, moist surface of moss. Rachel remembered the lessons of the woods that the boys had shared with her, including that moss grew on the north side of trees. If she went in the opposite direction, she should run into Camp Wellfleet.

Now all she had to do was steer a path through the quagmire. With the lantern held aloft, she headed off on a southerly route. She tried to jump to the next hummock. She hit the mark, but the slippery surface made her slide off into the smelly water. Rachel thought for a second about her new white Keds, probably only good for clam digging now. She waded to the next mound and pulled herself up. She thought she could see a possible path through a series of trees and humps that looked close enough together to form an escape route.

She hopped to the next tree and grabbed it with her left hand. She shuffled her feet to avoid sliding and stood at the edge of the outcropping of soggy land. The next landing spot required a jump. She made the leap, but her trailing foot snagged on something. The jangle of a bell broke the silence and she fell face first into the putrid liquid as the lantern flew from her hand. She came up sputtering and spitting out the foul water. For the first time that night, she felt like crying. Her anger at Peter had fueled her determination, but now she felt miserable, defeated and alone.

No . . . no . . . she would not let him get away with this. She would find her way out of here if she had to crawl or swim. Without the lantern, it was pitch black, but as her eyes adjusted the light from the full moon filtered into the dense swamp. She aimed her body toward the south and started the disgusting trek toward where she hoped she would find Camp Wellfleet.

*****

Peter threw the potato sack at the open door of his hideout, clenched his fists in anger and screamed, "Rachel, where are you?"

The dim light of the false dawn tinged the night sky. In half an hour, the real dawn would break around 5 a.m. He could go looking for her, but he had no idea which direction she had chosen. She didn't know the swamp and was probably floundering helplessly, scared and panicked. He could save her, or he might end up wandering around like a fool and wasting his time. How had she escaped, and how long had she been gone?

He shoved the door open as the useless hasp clattered against the wall. The flashlight told the story. Two 2x4s dangled uselessly from the top of the cage and the army cot was in ruins. The lantern was missing and the toolbox was open. The hatchet and pry-bar stared at him from the door entrance. He needed to think. The words of the Count of Monte Cristo rang in his ears, but this time it was in Rachel's voice, and her mocking words dripped with contempt, *"How did I escape? With difficulty. How did I plan this moment? With pleasure."*

Peter slumped against the wall. What was his answer to her taunting act of betrayal? *"There is no evil angel, but love."* Shakespeare always knew truth. Was this why he had never been in love? The line between love and hate was a thin fabric. He'd never risked it before, and now he knew why. She was as bad as all the rest of them. Yes, she had fooled him, tricked him into falling in love, thinking she was special and pure. If she made it out of the swamp, she would bring the other evil people. They would gang up against him as evil forces always do.

He took a deep breath and felt a surge of determination. Perhaps he had always known it would come down to a showdown like this. He reached for the shotgun, opened the box of ammunition and loaded two shells into the double barrel. Then he repeated the process with the .22 rifle and the .38 revolver. He shoved the .38 in the back of his pants, propped the .22 against the wall, laid the shotgun across his legs and waited.

The words of Julius Caesar spoke in the voice of his grandfather:

"Cowards die many times before their deaths
The valiant never taste of death but once."

Yes, Shakespeare was his guide. The bard never failed. His own mortality sometimes misinterpreted the words, but now his path and fate were clear.

*****

Private Henderson walked the north side of the base perimeter in battle fatigues and helmet, his M1 on his shoulder. The first hints of dawn revealed the outline of shrubs and trees. His feet moved forward in a marching cadence while his brain drifted in and out of a half-sleep. He shook his head to clear his thoughts. Guard duty again. He had pulled this task so many times he could do it in his sleep. No, that wasn't a good thought. He needed to stay alert. Sergeant Bowers always stressed how important guard duty was; the difference between life and death, he had said. Bowers should know after all his years in battle. Then he remembered: Bowers was dead.

He thought he heard a sound, something feeble, a bird maybe or a skunk or raccoon getting ready to wrap up their night's scavenging. He shivered; those little critters gave him the creeps, always skulking around, especially near the garbage dump. Something moved on the edge of the trees, something with bright colors. He shifted his weapon to the ready position.

"Halt, who goes there?"

A soft voice replied, "Help me, please help me."

*****

Rob slept fitfully on the couch. He twitched and jumped at every sound as he fought exhaustion. He was terrified. The true love of his life was missing, and he had no idea what to do. His fear and anger wanted to explode, but there was no target for it. After twelve years of separation and blaming himself for his stupid behavior, he was reunited with Rachel. *Now what?* He knew he couldn't lose her again.

A ringing buzzed in his dreams. Wait, it was that stupid phone. Maybe Rachel? He stumbled to his feet and grabbed the receiver.

"Hello . . . Hello?"

A tired voice replied, "Rob, it's me, Rachel. I'm safe and at the infirmary at Camp Wellfleet. I was . . . it was . . ." she broke into sobs.

Another voice entered the call. "Hi, Rob, it's George. Rachel is going to be fine: exhausted, dehydrated, and scratched up a bit. With rest she'll be good as new."

"George, I'm on my way. You can fill me in when I get there. Do we know who did it? Was it that college teacher?"

"Yes, it was."

"I'm leaving now." He grabbed his wrinkled uniform off the floor. Time to be a police officer again.

*****

"Bound Brook Police. How may I help you? Hello, George. Oh, you found her? Thank goodness! No, Chief Foster isn't here, but Trooper O'Connor is. Yes, we got a call from Chief Berrio in Truro that someone remembered the owner of that vehicle. It's the grandson of old Hermit Higgins, so he and Skip left to help the Truro police. I guess old H.H. kept some guns in the house, so they are being careful, in case the grandson is there with Rachel."

"Ask him where they are," snarled O'Connor. "Here let me talk to him."

"Tell me what you know. . . . okay, right, right, I got it. I'm on my way. In a swamp you said, the white cedar swamp. . . Near Camp Wellfleet . . . She thinks he killed the army sergeant . . . Okay, sit tight." O'Connor hung up the phone.

"Hey, you weren't supposed to hang up," snapped Diane.

O'Connor waved a dismissive hand. "Never mind, you have a map? Where is this place?"

Diane pointed to the large national survey maps on the wall. "All the maps from P'town to Orleans. The swamp is on the Wellfleet one, just north of the army camp."

O'Connor gave the map a glance, grabbed his hat and headed for the door.

"Hey wait, don't you think you should talk to the Chief?" Too late, the trooper was gone. All she heard was the sound of his boots pounding down the long stairway.

O'Connor switched on the cruiser's lights and siren as he peeled out of the station. He wasn't waiting for anyone. This was his chance to make a major arrest. If he waited for the police chiefs, they would give him something minor to do, and they'd take all the credit. It was his good luck that Corporal Stewart was at his grandmother's funeral services. *Wait until my father hears about this!* Man, it will make him proud. The cruiser sped onto the highway and flew down Route 6, hitting ninety miles an hour.

*****

"Chief Berrio, Chief Fleming," said Foster, "that was my dispatcher. Rachel Curtis is safe at Camp Wellfleet. The professor kidnapped her. He's the grandson of Hermit. He held her prisoner in some kind of cabin in the White Cedar Swamp. Rachel thinks he killed the army sergeant, so he may be a murderer as well as a kidnapper."

The police officers from Truro, Wellfleet and Bound Brook gathered around him. "Well, we know our suspect isn't here now, but it looks like someone was here not too long ago," said Berrio. "I know that old Hermie had a shotgun and .22 rifle and we didn't find them. So, our suspect might be armed."

Bill Fleming looked at Foster. "Wellfleet is my town, so I'm on my way." He turned to Paul Lussier and Pheeny Rego, "You men come with me."

Foster nodded. "And I'm going too. I'll take Skip. Chief Berrio, I think you and your men better secure this scene, and be here in case he tries to come back."

"Diane also told me that Trooper O'Connor already left. Bill, we better move fast, because I don't trust that kid."

Chapter 30

*"When sorrows come, they come not in single spies,
but in battalions."*
William Shakespeare – Hamlet: Act 4, Scene 5

Dawn, Tuesday, July 8th

Rob slowed at the Camp Wellfleet gate.

The guard recognized his uniform, "Go ahead, they've been expecting you," he yelled as Rob picked up speed.

At the infirmary, he jumped out of his truck and ran inside. "Where is she?"

"Rob, I'm over here." Her voice came from behind a hospital partition. He pushed the partition aside and saw Rachel in bed, wearing a hospital johnny.

She reached her arms and he bent down and grabbed her in a bear hug. "Easy, lover boy, I'm a little tender in a few spots."

"I was so worried . . . Are you okay? . . . What happened? . . . And where is he?" The last question was through gritted teeth.

Rachel freed herself from his embrace and settled back on the pillow. She sighed, "Well, here is the short version; maybe my Dad can tell you the rest. Dr. Peter Burke drugged me and somehow took me into the cedar swamp. He has a little shelter he built in the middle of it, and he put me in a wooden cage. He left last night and I managed to pry apart the bars, chop open the door and escape. Then I had to slog through the swamp until I found Camp Wellfleet.

"He came back though. I heard him scream my name when I was near the edge of the swamp. Listen to me; be careful, I think he killed Sergeant Bowers. I saw bloodstains on a 2x4. He's dangerous. I mean he's completely crazy!"

Rob squeezed her hand. "Don't worry, we'll find him. You're safe now. You need rest."

Maggie Gilmore gave Rob a hug. "We're so glad you're here."

George shook his hand. "I can tell you more later, but our daughter is quite the determined prisoner. That professor had no idea who he was dealing with."

"Oh Dad, I just used some of the things I learned growing up in Bound Brook, hanging out with the guys. Now if you will all forgive me, I need to sleep."

Maggie kissed her daughter's forehead. "You do that, honey. I'm just going to sit right here beside the bed."

George gestured Rob toward the door. "Let me fill you in."

Outside, they ran into Captain Anderson. "Mr. Gilmore, the Colonel has ordered the sentry guard detail to be tripled, and they all have live ammunition. It's only the regular army platoon, none of the national guard. Don't think he fully trusts the reservists. Anyway, if that man tries to escape through the camp, he'll be spotted and dealt with."

Anderson looked at Rob and extended his hand. "Captain Ray Anderson, sir."

"Rob Caldwell, I'm a special on the Bound Brook Police Force . . . and also, Rachel is my girlfriend."

"Oh, I see. Well, congratulations, y'all are a lucky man."

"Captain, can you tell us what is happening?" asked George.

"Yes, sir, the Colonel asked me to bring y'all up to speed. The Bound Brook Police and Wellfleet Police are on the way, but they are out in some remote place in the town called

Truro. I guess somebody reported that the man lived there. So might take them a while."

Before he finished, a state police cruiser came roaring down the road with lights flashing and siren screeching. It skidded to a stop and a trooper leaped out. "Which way is the man's location?" he barked.

"Hello, Trooper O'Connor," said Rob. "I think the Bound Brook and Wellfleet Police will be here any minute. I'm sure you'll want to coordinate with them."

"No time for that. The suspect could be making his get-away as we speak. Where did the woman say he is? Did I hear it was in a swamp?"

"Yes, he has a camouflaged shelter he built in the middle of the swamp," said George.

"Did the woman say he was armed?"

George shook his head. "Rachel said he wasn't armed when she saw him last. Listen, we don't even know if he's there."

O'Connor turned toward Anderson, noticing the two silver bars on his collar, "Captain, can you show me the location where she was found?"

"I sure can. Follow me." The two men headed off at a fast pace and disappeared behind the infirmary.

Rob looked at George. "I don't know about you, but I'm going after him too."

A voice yelled, "What's going on?" Simon Eldredge was walking up the road, half-awake, barefoot and disheveled.

George waved. "Simon, why are you here so early?"

"I slept in the PX last night. I was here late and decided to stay over. Made a bed out of the boxes in the storage area."

"The man who kidnapped Rachel is in the swamp," said George. "The state trooper has gone in after him. We're going to help. Do us a favor, go in the infirmary and tell my wife what's going on."

Rob broke into a jog, with George following close behind. Simon watched them disappear around the building. The old Simon would have just talked to George's wife and waited here, wringing his hands and leaving it to the authorities. The new Simon wanted to be part of the action.

*****

Simon stuck his head in the infirmary. "Mrs. Gilmore, hello."

"Yes, I'm back here."

"Your husband and Rob are going to help the state trooper. I can't stay; I'm going to go help out too." With the last words, Simon turned and hurried back to the PX as fast as his bare feet would allow. At the store, he scrambled into his shoes and socks. Then he paused and thought about his 5' 8" 135 pound build; he needed a weapon. In the sporting goods section, he grabbed the Stan "The Man" Musial model Louisville Slugger.

Outside he paused and then started toward the thick trees to the north. A jogging figure in uniform emerged from the shrubs.

"Captain Anderson, is that you?"

"Yes, Mr. Eldredge. I'm not authorized to help the state trooper, but I'm going to see Colonel Murphy and ask if he will give me permission to take a squad to join the search."

"Did you see George and Rob?"

"Yes, they're trying to catch up to the policeman."

"Which way did they go?"

"Follow the path, but I didn't go very far. I had to turn back before the real swamp, so I can't tell you much. Excuse me, sir, I've got to hurry." The Captain double-timed it toward the headquarters building.

Simon hustled toward the shrubs and followed a path into the woods. The path gradually descended as the vegetation changed from scrub pines, bayberry bushes and shrubs, to hard wood trees and crowberry ground cover. After a quarter-mile he came to a fork in the path. Which way? He went to the right.

He started to get discouraged when the path disappeared into a soggy marsh. He hesitated at the edge of the water. No doubt, he was going to get wet. Then he heard shouts, the state trooper yelling warnings.

Boom! A shot echoed through the trees, the deep-throated roar of a shotgun. The shot seemed to come from all directions and gave Simon no clue to its source. Then a scream. He almost lost his nerve, a chill made him shiver. He inhaled and reminded himself that the old Simon was gone. This was the new Simon. He stepped into the water, made a choice and slogged forward.

*****

Trooper O'Connor jumped over a black pool of swamp water to a hummock of wet grass. He grabbed a tree to keep his balance and squinted into the dim light of the marsh. He had no idea where he was going. Maybe he should have thought this out better. Too late now, he was committed. When he had doubts, O'Connor's practice was to plunge in and push ahead. Doubts were for cowards.

"Professor, this is the Massachusetts State Police, come out with your hands up."

His words were swallowed by the thick vegetation and humid air. He drew his service revolver from its holster.

"Professor, don't make it harder on yourself. I'm armed, and will not hesitate to shoot if you force me to."

His answer was heavy silence. O'Connor continued on his course and jumped to the next clump surrounding a cedar. He thought he could make out a pathway, a vaguely suggested route. Then he saw it. There was a large mound covered in vegetation that protruded from the bog. It looked natural in origin, but was much taller than the surrounding area. He picked up his pace and leaped to the next grassy outcrop.

"Professor, I'm giving you one last chance, this is your final warning. Surrender and you won't get hurt."

Still silence. O'Connor crouched and scanned the surrounding area. It looked like five or six more jumps and he would be at his goal. He pushed off, but his foot caught and he tumbled into the thick sludge. His revolver and uniform hat went flying. A bell jangled and then came a thunderous *Boom*! The leaves rustled from a sudden gust of air and pellets smacked into the closest tree. A shotgun blast.

He tried to free himself from the disgusting muck, but then the pain hit him hard. He screamed in agony as he reached for his right leg. He trembled and bit down hard. His fingers felt down to his right calf and around to the shinbone. An odd bump protruded under his uniform trousers, a bump that shouldn't have been there. The pain numbed his muscles and left him too stunned to move.

A voice came from his right. "Don't come any closer. I'm a crack-shot, and I missed on purpose. Like you said, *this is your final warning.*"

Then O'Connor heard a laugh, a weird cackle that seemed to fit in the spooky setting.

*****

George and Rob followed the sounds of O'Connor's voice as he yelled warnings to Burke. He sounded close.

Boom! Rob flinched and ducked. He looked at George, who stooped low. Then came a blood-curdling scream.

He whispered, "George, the trooper didn't have a shotgun that I know of. We've got to assume that the professor is armed, and O'Connor is hurt."

"I think I saw something, a quick movement of the leaves up ahead. I hope the trooper wasn't shot."

Then they heard a voice: "Don't come any closer. I'm a crack shot, I missed on purpose. Like you said, *this is your final warning.*" Then a strange laugh that sent goose bumps down Rob's spine.

"Psst, Rob, he doesn't know we're here. I'm going to crawl ahead to that spot where I saw the leaves move. I think the trooper might be there. Can you go around to the right? It sounded like the voice came from that direction. Maybe you can distract the professor while I check on O'Connor. Keep low; I guess I don't need to tell you to be careful. If we can buy some time, there should be help on the way, but the trooper may need medical help before they get here."

He watched Rob make his way to the right, keeping low and moving silently. Then George slithered into the slimy water trying to avoid splashing sounds. He could hear moaning groans straight ahead and pushed forward.

"Help, I broke my leg. I need help."

*****

Simon couldn't place the direction of the sounds, but his best guess was that they came from the left. He started angling that way as the water rose from ankle-deep to mid-calf. He considered trying to get on the tufts of grassy hummocks, but he was afraid it would make him a better target for whoever fired the shot. Then an anguished voice called out, *"Help, I broke my leg. I need help."* Now he was sure the sound was more to the left.

The swamp grew thicker and light became dim. He was starting to question his decision when he heard a movement. Something or someone was slowly pushing through the water ahead. Simon decided to follow the sound.

*****

Peter waited on a large hummock twenty-five feet from his hideout as he reloaded the shotgun. He had known his enemies would focus on his fortress and had decided to flank them. The policeman never saw him, so he guessed the strategy had worked. After the man screamed that his leg was broken, he continued to hear his low moans and whimpers. He didn't hear anyone else, but he knew there would be more of them coming. Now, his anger and his resolve both faded. The little voice in the back of his head tried to push forward, asking him, *What are you doing?* He waited for the louder voice to answer with a strong quote from Shakespeare, but it was silent.

He snatched his shotgun and .22 rifle, stood and jumped to the next mound. A sudden sense of urgency, a primal need to protect his fortress, drove him forward. He threw aside any attempt at stealth; his breathing was labored and the footsteps loud and hurried. The quotes were gone, replaced by jumbled pieces of literature involving battles, sieges and walled castles. Here, at his citadel, Peter would make his stand.

He stood in front of his small fort, the work of his own hands, and wished his grandfather could see it now. Old H.H. had always known the truth: the world was never fair. He realized now too late he didn't need Shakespeare, Homer or any other writer. All he had ever needed was his grandfather.

He felt sick, as a nauseous bile rose in his throat. *Was this it? Was this all there was to his life?* He searched in vain for some guidance, for some wisdom or advice. Nothing came to his panicked mind. He pointed the shotgun toward the sky and fired both barrels. *Boom! Boom!* Then the gangster voice of the actor James Cagney rose from his lips in an anguished scream, *"Come and get me, coppers!"*

*****

Rob was almost there. He had spotted Peter as he moved from his sniper perch back to his hideout. He circled behind him and watched his bizarre behavior unfold. The professor shook his head as if bewildered, then jumped from foot to foot as if undecided where he should go. Rob became less concerned about noise as he realized that Peter was in some sort of trance. He watched as Burke pointed the shotgun in the air, and he flinched as both barrels exploded. The eerie voice shrieked out with a classic movie line, *"Come and get me, coppers!"*

Rob saw his chance. He pushed through the water to the back of the mound, grabbed the trunk of a cedar and pulled himself up. The back of the camouflaged shack blocked his view of Peter. Dripping and covered in slime, he moved along the wall and burst into the open. Burke spun, pointed the shotgun and pulled both triggers. *Click! Click!*

Rob leaped forward in a low crouch. Burke grabbed the shotgun barrel and swung at the charging figure. The wooden stock swished past Rob's head, but clipped his right ear before flying through the air into the water. He hit Burke in the midsection with his right shoulder and they both tumbled to the slippery surface with Rob on top. He fought against the stinging pain and pressed his advantage.

Burke squirmed and tried to roll away. Rob used the momentum to turn him onto his stomach and slide both hands under Peter's armpits and up behind his neck, lacing his fingers together to complete a full-nelson wrestling hold. With Burke now immobilized, Rob knelt, put one knee on the professor's spine and pulled back until he heard a squeal of pain.

"If you try to fight it, the pain will be worse. I need you to get on your knees and then stand up. You are under arrest."

Burke staggered to his feet, then twisted and squirmed. Rob felt his grip slipping, the slimy ooze on his hands and clothes slick and greasy. Burke slid through his grasp, spun and pulled away toward the shack. The professor fumbled for something behind his back as Rob lunged at his legs. His right foot slipped on the slick surface and he landed sprawled in the muck.

"Don't move!"

Rob looked up to see Burke holding a .38 service revolver.

"I recognize you. You're the boyfriend. Well, if I can't have her, then you won't either."

Then George yelled, "Professor, don't do it. I have you covered."

"You're a liar. I saw the trooper's gun go flying, and if you had a gun you would have fired it by now. You're just trying to distract me."

Rob held his breath and braced for the inevitable, but a movement caught his eye. A slim figure crept along the side of the hut behind Burke.

"I know I'm a goner. I don't think I ever have fit in this world anyway. But, before I go, you are going with me." He raised the revolver and cocked the hammer. "Perhaps I'll see you in Valhalla or Heaven, or more likely in Hell."

Simon leapt forward, his arm raised high wielding the Louisville Slugger. Peter heard the sound. He tried to spin, but he was too late. The bat crashed down on his skull and the .38 fell from his grip. As he staggered, Simon delivered the "coup de grace," a full right-hand fungo swing that caught Burke in the right temple. The force drove him off his feet and his body landed in the murky water.

Rob exhaled and looked up at the skinny PX manager. Simon's face had a strange aura, a look of rapture or shock, he couldn't tell which. "Thank you, Simon. You saved my life. He was going to shoot me."

Simon gave Rob a dazed look. "I just did what had to be done. He deserved it. My father always said, *You shall reap what you sow.*"

Chapter 31
Revelations

Tomorrow, and tomorrow, and tomorrow
Creeps in this petty pace from day to day,
To the last syllable of recorded time;
And all our yesterdays have lighted fools
The way to dusty death. Out, out, brief candle!
Life's but a walking shadow, a poor player,
That struts and frets his hour upon the stage,
And then is heard no more. It is a tale
Told by an idiot, full of sound and fury,
Signifying nothing.
William Shakespeare – Macbeth: Act 5, Scene 5

Within minutes, the area was swarming with people. First, the Bound Brook and Wellfleet police arrived with revolvers drawn, shouting warnings and trying to make sense of the scene. Then a squad of army soldiers surrounded the area. Somehow, amid the confusion, Trooper O'Connor was taken for medical treatment, Burke's lifeless body was removed and Rob, George and Simon were escorted back to the Camp Wellfleet HQ. The PX became the command center for the investigation. Simon, Rob and George gave their statements to Chief Foster and Chief Fleming. The morning flew by in a flash.

Rob went back to the infirmary to check on Rachel. Maggie saw him and held up one finger. "Give her a minute, she's getting dressed. The doctor says she is fine to go home."

The partition curtain pushed back and Rachel flew into his arms. "Thank God, you're alright! I was so scared. Is it true that maniac almost shot you?"

"I'm fine, thanks to Simon."

The couple locked into a deep kiss and embrace.

"Why don't you two get out of here?" laughed Maggie.

Rachel grabbed Rob's hand and led him out of the infirmary. They ran into George outside the door. He pointed toward the PX. "Looks like the big cheese has arrived."

A cluster of state police cruisers were parked beside the Post Exchange. An older state trooper with a command braid on his uniform was in a heated conversation with Chiefs Foster and Fleming. They were too far away to hear the words, but it was obvious that Foster and the trooper were angry, while Fleming just shook his head in disgust. Other troopers were keeping a respectful distance.

"So, Rob, do you know what that is all about?"

Rob laughed. "I have a feeling that Trooper O'Connor's father has arrived and taken command. He and Bull Foster have a bad history, and it looks like it's getting even worse."

Foster took off his hat and slapped it against his leg in a show of frustration. Then he turned on his heel and stormed back toward the PX, followed by a glum-looking Chief Fleming. The trooper turned and pointed to a civilian car. He gestured for the driver to come over. The car door opened and two men got out. The driver carried a notepad, while the passenger pulled camera equipment out of the back seat. Rob spotted the lettering on the car door: *Boston Record American.*

"Looks like the newspaper reporter is here and getting an exclusive. Probably be interesting to see what version of the story is printed. I have a feeling it will be different than the version Foster and Fleming would tell."

A young trooper exited the PX and escorted Simon over to the reporter and cameraman. Simon carried the baseball bat over his shoulder.

George laughed. "Well, good for Simon. I guess he gets to be a hero. Hope it finally makes his father proud."

*****

Simon returned to the PX after his newspaper interview. Rob went over and shook his hand.

"Before we leave, I needed to thank you one more time for what you did. Man, you showed up just in time!"

Simon looked bewildered. "Gee, I don't know what to say. I'm still in a state of shock. They wanted to take my picture. I guess I'm just glad I could help."

"Simon, I never knew you were so good with a bat," said George. "Maybe we should have had you on the baseball team."

Simon looked at George and his eyes drifted off. "Funny, I can't hit a pitched ball, but I spent hours hitting fungos to my brothers. When I saw this bat in the delivery, it was like it was meant for me. Stan Musial is my favorite player. All my brothers love Ted Williams and the Red Sox, but I guess I needed my own star player. Maybe it was my little rebellion."

He patted the bat's label, then walked over and put it back in the display.

"No," George shook his head, "you need to keep that bat. It's not for sale. I'll buy it for you. It's yours."

"I appreciate that. Yes, I guess it's too used to sell, anyway." He plucked it out of the rack and took a practice swing. "It's more than a baseball bat. I think it was sent to me for a purpose. My father taught us all to fight evil, and I guess that's what I did. You know, when I hit that man it felt like someone else was guiding my aim. It was like I was outside my body watching it happen. I knew I had to do it fast or he was going to shoot Rob."

Rachel walked over and gave him a hug. "Thank goodness you were there, Simon. You really are a hero."

He flushed. "Gee, thank you, Rachel.

"Ditto from me," George added.

"You know, it doesn't seem real. George, do you mind if I go back to my place? It's been a long day, and I think I'm still in shock."

George nodded. "Sure, Simon. We're not opening the store today. Go rest up."

The three watched him walk out the door with the bat slung over his shoulder. He seemed like he was in a daze.

Rob looked at George. "You know, one thing still bothers me."

"What's that?"

"Well, we are assuming that the professor murdered Sergeant Bowers. It makes sense, and it's very likely that he did, but we don't really have any evidence."

George nodded. "You're right, Rob. However, the police already have their murderer and they also have their hero. You saw that argument between Chief Foster and Trooper O'Connor's father. That reporter and photographer weren't there by coincidence. As far as the state police are concerned, Burke killed Bowers because of what he did to Rachel. He was crazy.

"He kidnapped Rachel with some delusion that she loved him. Then he was a heartbeat away from killing you. The trooper is a hero and Simon saved the day. The story is told and the ending is complete. You may have your doubts, but the DA and the state police have closed the case and they are moving on. Now all the rest of us get to live happily ever after."

*****

Simon walked to his borrowed car and opened the door. He patted his trusty Louisville Slugger before tossing the bat onto the passenger seat. It was the second time the bat had come in handy.

He felt numb as if someone else was moving his arms and legs as he climbed behind the wheel. The events of the past few days started to swirl in his brain. The newspaperman had called him a hero and said it would be in the paper. For one of the few times in his life he had acted on instinct. He had seen Burke point the gun at Rob and he had reacted.

It wasn't like the first time. He flashed back to that night in Provincetown. Each evening he had followed the Sergeant, he had become angrier. Bowers strutted around the town, flirting with women and making deals with shady men. He couldn't prove it, but he knew Bowers was selling the stolen PX goods.

That final night he had realized just how evil the man was, and he had known what had to be done. When he watched Bowers leave the Mayflower with that woman, it gave him a bad feeling. He had followed the Jeep, but parked down a dirt road off to the side and waited. Then the big man named Moose had pulled up in his pickup truck and he had heard the woman yell.

He had watched the truck leave but remained frozen with indecision. Then his father's face had appeared before him, sneering, mocking and calling him worthless. He had grabbed the Stan Musial bat from the back seat and headed toward the pond.

His father's words had resounded in his brain: *"Nobody steals from an Eldredge!"*

Chapter 32

"All's Well That Ends Well"
William Shakespeare

Rachel sat in a folding beach chair outside Rob's cottage and watched the setting sun spread a crimson glow over Bound Brook Bay. Rob dozed in another chair, his head flopping up and down as he slipped in and out of consciousness. It made a comical scene, with his long body trying to curl up in the small canvas chair.

The sound of tires crunching on the shell driveway broke the spell. A shiny blue car parked behind Rachel's DeSoto and Jimmy opened the door. He gave Rachel a sheepish wave.

"Rob, wake up." She stood up, ran to Jimmy's arms and wrapped him in an embrace. "Thank God, they let you out."

"Well, you guys solved the murder, and I guess being drunk wasn't enough for them to keep me locked up."

"Hey there, Jimmy! Good to see you." Rob shook his hand, but Jim pulled him into the three-person hug. "You two are the best friends any man ever had. I don't know what I did to deserve you, but I'm going to do my best to be worth it."

He pulled away and went back to the car. "Doubt you've seen this special evening edition. Just arrived from Boston." He handed them a newspaper and pointed to the story and picture on the front page. In the photo, Simon Eldredge smiled meekly as he shouldered his bat.

Deranged Murderer Stopped by Hero Trooper
Exclusive to the Record American – Evening Edition
By Jeff White

A violent drama took place this morning in Wellfleet on Cape Cod. Peter Burke, an instructor at Boston University, kidnapped a local woman and is believed to have murdered a soldier stationed at Camp Wellfleet. A rescue party led by State Trooper Michael O'Connor arrived just in time to prevent a second murder. The crazed killer had his gun pointed at a local police officer before O'Connor and civilian Simon Eldredge subdued the culprit. In the ensuing scuffle, Burke was killed and Trooper O'Connor received a broken leg.

It is believed that the crazed intellectual was obsessively jealous of the local woman he had kidnapped. State Police believe he also killed Sergeant Theodore Bowers, a decorated war veteran. The decisive action by Trooper O'Connor solved a murder, kidnapping and prevented a second murder.

O'Connor praised the help of Simon Eldredge, the manager of the Camp Wellfleet Post Exchange. "Mr. Eldredge's assistance was critically helpful to me in stopping this dangerous criminal's crime spree." Eldredge used a baseball bat to disarm the culprit. The modest PX manager had only a few words. "I just did what needed to be done. My father taught me that no wrong deed should go unpunished."

O'Connor will receive a departmental award for his heroic action.

The End

Acknowledgments

Many people have contributed to this book and my journey as a writer. The town of Wellfleet and its people are the inspiration that keeps me writing. My wife, Ellen Keane, provides the first critique of my drafts. She is an astute reader—an honest and sometimes brutal critic—just what a writer needs. Her comments are always on the mark. If she likes it, then I know it is good.

The Cape Cod Writers Center has been a wonderful resource and support system. The CCWC has provided me with years of workshops, presentations, advice, fellowship and networking.

Steve Trinward of "Trinwords" has been my final editor for both Bound Brook books. Steve cleans up my grammar and punctuation, as well as providing insights into characterization. Any mistakes that slip through are a result of my own last minute tinkering. I know; I should leave well enough alone.

A special thanks to my brother-in-law, Jack Delaney. Jack is my early-round editor, whose sharp eye for detail cleans up the first drafts. He is also a Korean War army veteran who has provided key insights into the era.

Jim Hooker's father was a sergeant at Camp Wellfleet. Sergeant Hooker was an honorable soldier and a veteran of the D-Day Landing. He would never have tolerated Ted Bowers. Jim worked at the Camp Wellfleet PX in the summer of 1957 with my father, Wellfleet Principal Dick Cochran, and he gave me details about the store. Andy Pierce checked my descriptions of the White Cedar Swamp and Arty Parker contributed details on volunteer fire department procedures. Irene Herlihy was my BETA reader of the preview copy. A belated thank you goes to Alan Schlesinger, who did extensive editing and feedback on my first novel, *Murder at Bound Brook*. Thanks go to Dorothy Bayne, my writing group partner who served as a great sounding board for this book.

Wellfleet friends have been great resources, cheerleaders and supporters. Thank you to David Wright, Jeff Tash, Vern Costa, Ron Stewart, Geoff Kane, Jeff White, Suzanne Grout Thomas, Stephen Russell, David Weintraub and many others. Writer friends Jim Coogan, Ray Anderson and Steve Marini have served as role models and mentors.

In Provincetown, the Mayflower Café and Old Colony Tap are town institutions. Thanks to Darin Janoplis for back history on the Mayflower and its layout in 1952. Most of the Wellfleet and Truro people in the book are real. However, the Bound Brook people are all fictitious.

Camp Wellfleet was decommissioned in 1960. It is now the headquarters of the Cape Cod National Seashore. The Marconi Wireless site and the Atlantic White Cedar Swamp are real locations that are part of the National Seashore. Information about the Marconi site is preserved, but erosion washed the towers into the ocean years ago. You can visit the Atlantic White Cedar Swamp without getting your feet wet. A boardwalk guides you safely through the bog. It is an interesting walk, but bring the bug spray.

I hope to continue the Bound Brook series. I want to know what happens to Rob, Rachel, Jimmy, Moose, Elaine and the rest of the characters. They have become real members of my extended family and I hope you feel that way about them too.